ELAINE CORREIA

LESSONS

FOR THE

GODDESS BORN

THE REBEL HEALERS
MYSTIC'S GUIDE TO YOUR PURPOSEE AND INNER MAGIC

Book Cover and illustrations by Elaine Correia

Inner Wisdom

PO Box 840

Waldport, OR 97394

Print ISBN: 978-0-9831370-5-4

Ebook ISBN: 978-0-9831370-4-7

Illuminating Inner Wisdom

CONTENTS

PREFACE

Writing the first book in *The Rebel Healers* fantasy series invited me to become more than I thought I could be. I reawakened the part of myself that had been abandoned and displaced when I took on the responsibilities of a husband, children, and multiple businesses, as well as trying to fit into society's expectations of a wife, mother, and entrepreneur. Like my main character Ellara, each of us has a deeper potential and purpose that we often dare not give ourselves permission to embrace until we are older, when the heroine's journey of our soul begins in earnest.

I became completely absorbed in writing *The Rebel Healers* series. I spent hours thinking about the storyline, the environment, Ellara's and Rokan's magic, and the social atmosphere in which the story took place. The tone, rhythm, and word choices of the people around me, along with what they looked like and how they responded to situations, anchored my descriptions. The sensations of the wind and the rain on my body, as well as messages carried on the wind whistling through the trees, expanded my awareness and, hence, the fictional world I created. I wondered how my characters would respond to my life's situations. Gradually, the Rebel Healers' challenges became a representation of the quest for love, safety, survival, and finding meaning in life that we face every day.

Ellara's world became a mirror of ours, reflecting patriarchal dominance, disrespect and subjugation of women, overuse of planet resources, and lack of spiritual connection.

Ellara's story reveals the disruption to her peaceful home by Natuan clerics and their mercenaries, who attempt to impose a patriarchal rule. Aided by the Droc'ri sorcerers and their greedy Grand Master who wants to rule their world, they hunt and kill the Healers and destroy women's freedoms and businesses. Ellara must rise to defend her homeland and unmask and declaw the perpetrators before she can restore balance in her world. But it is not a simple task, and she has to become more than she thinks she is. To survive, she must learn to trust herself and her abilities, and discern who is friend or foe. You're invited to read her story and become inspired by how she navigates the challenges she faces.

After I finished writing *The Rebel Healers,* I was inspired to offer my readers the opportunity to bring Ellara's world into their lives. Use her wisdom to tackle your struggles and find peace by balancing the light and dark within you and the world. As a Healer not traditionally trained, what better person to invite my readers to free themselves from their constraints and status quo, and to see their lives from a new perspective?

In this companion guide, Ellara takes you into her world and shares her insights and the practices she used to become a proficient Healer. Through discussions with Cleric Paul and guidance from Nana Magog, Ellara formed her own understanding of the Goddess's teachings and Gra'Bandia tradition. Her intention with this guide is to awaken and nudge others along a fulfilling path that will restore balance and harmony in one's daily life, the world, and the planet. She invites us to let her words bridge the worlds so we, too, can become Healers that bring forth a new dawn that benefits all.

Within these pages, Ellara invites you to examine your life and see how doubts and fears restrict you. Reclaim the part of yourself that you have suppressed or denied for the sake of fitting in and being accepted by society. Gather the bits and pieces of your soul. Connect to your true essence, which permeates your life, whether or not you are aware of it. Satisfy an inner longing to be part of something bigger. Listen to the calling of your heart and soul to make a difference in the world. Answer the call of your destiny and do your part to rebalance and restore harmony in your life and our world.

The organization of the handbook provides you with topics for contemplation. They begin with a fable followed by Ellara's comments. The next section is about applying Ellara's wisdom. As the author, I suggest practices to do and prompts upon which to journal. I have separated the sections with symbols that represent each narrator.

Take all the time you need to work through the sections. Ellara's stories will have more meaning if you have read *The Rebel Healers,* but you can use this companion book as a stand-alone guide as well.

You're invited to join Ellara in the Heartland Forest of Gea. Enjoy the Leonini fables Cleric Paul translated from the forgotten Goddess manuscripts. Consider all she has to say and become inspired by what she shares.

Ellara's Invitation

"Welcome, Goddess-born. I have called you together because the balance of power between the light and dark has shifted. I need your help in battling the threat of darkness invading our world."

With a steady pace, I stroll along the circle of women, reading the determination in their dirt-smudged faces. Their pair'ti mates sit beside them, and others sit behind them. I exhale slowly, searching for the best words to convey my message. "Please give me the words that will awaken understanding," I whisper to the Goddess.

"Sinister forces are determined to dominate our world, force their restrictive patriarchal beliefs on us, silently steal our freedoms, and force us into unwelcome servitude. Through trickery, they now control much of the world.

"They see Healers, the keepers of the Divine Light, as a threat. Our forces of light can unravel the dark organization's plans. That is why those in the shadows intend to silence the Healers. To members of this nefarious organization, everything is black and white. If a person does not support them, they become their enemy. They cannot see other possibilities. Clouded by the fear their dark masters feed upon, they cannot know that they need the Healers to survive and thrive. It is the very light we work with that they need to live. By the same token, we need the dark energies they manifest to prod us forward on our mystical journey. Each polarity serves a purpose. It's essential to maintain a balance.

A pitch pocket from a spruce limb explodes in the fire, and a cloud of sparks scatters upward, disappearing into the night. Startled gasps escape from my listeners, followed by nervous chuckles.

"These shadowy persons are not omnipotent," I continue after all the glowing embers vanish. "It's within our power to stop the rise in chaos and the darkness that eats away at our hearts. We are more powerful than we think. We must step into our gifts and reclaim our inner power and sovereignty.

"We live in a challenging time. The agents of darkness sow chaos and fight to keep their way of life. The leader of the Gra'Bandia Council aids those destructive forces in our world. She adheres to an outdated tradition formed centuries ago. This is understandable, as it is easy to get trapped in fixed thinking patterns—believing one ideology to be correct because it is the only way it has ever been. This is a fallacy. There are many solutions.

"An unconventional group of Healers needs to emerge to overcome this situation. It takes someone not steeped in a rigid tradition— a rebel—to create anew. As revolutionary Healers, we have an advantage. We can look at a situation with fresh eyes, not yet shaped by a fixed mode of behavior. In our Divinely guided innocence, we can discover new responses to the ominous incursion and compose new interpretations of the ancient manuscripts. That is why I called you."

"But we don't have the powers of a Healer," one woman says. Other voices joined her. "How can we make a difference? The forces we face are far beyond what we can do."

Someone else says, "We don't know what we can do. We are not trained."

I nod. "I was not formally trained as a Gra'Bandia Healer. In light of the Droc'ri threat, my mother, who disapproved of my healing ability, tried to discourage me from using it. Nana Magog was not much help in my younger years but taught me just enough to awaken my talent. Unlike other narrow-minded clergymen, Cleric Paul presented me with esoteric teachings of the Leonini Codes written long before the Gra'Bandia Council was formed. The myths and parables within the codes illustrated a way of seeing the world from a different viewpoint, and their ideals gave me a vision of what a Healer is. By restricting my exposure to Doyen Camila and the Gra'Bandia Council's limited vision of a Healer, Nana Magog, and my mother did me a service, leaving me free to make new interpretations of the ancient wisdom. I offer you my wisdom and practices so that you can become the powerful person you are."

I circle the group again, listening with my inner awareness of how to help them overcome their doubts.

"I had to learn about my talents on my own. Contrary to what I imagined, I discovered the role of a Healer is not to fix a situation or a person. Instead, healing means to make whole, and the Healer's role is to create an energetic opening where the person or persons involved can make a different choice. There is no fixing or forcing your will on another or in a situation. A Healer's role is to facilitate change and accept what unfolds. Thus, Healers illuminate the darkness.

"A Healer becomes a wise leader and guardian of her people. She will defend them as pacifically as possible. She uses her power wisely and sparingly. The biggest gift she can give to another is the freedom to choose. The more she works with the Goddess's Love and Light, the more she becomes a bridge between the physical and unseen worlds. At the heart of it, we are all children of the Goddess.

"The greatest weapon the Healer has against a dark threat is a deep knowing of herself and a strong connection to her spirit. When you know you *are* Divine Love and Light, anything less than this frequency cannot stand before it. I will show you how you can connect strongly to your soul."

"But Ellara, you have been doing this for years. We are new to this. How can we learn what we need to know in such a short time?"

Touching her shoulder and smiling, I say, "The first step is to overcome the belief that you do not possess the ability." I sweep my arm around those gathered. "You are here. You have the ability. Each and every one of you. In fact, you use your natural abilities every day.

Become aware of how you use your natural talents, and you will see you are more capable and powerful than you think."

I hear murmurs of assent and heads nod.

"Most of the practices I am about to share with you I learned from years of trial and error. Together, we can grow and expand our innate powers and abilities, awaken love in our hearts and the hearts of others, and cast out the shadows of fear and mistrust. We will regain our sovereignty, and our world will thrive again.

"These practices will be easier if you approach them with an open mind and heart and are willing to face whatever the Goddess wishes you to know. We must explore what is possible and what appears impossible to address the dark threat. This may mean journeying into other realms and out of your comfort zone.

"It helps to understand more about yourself and some factors that are perceived as limitations. Some of you are highly sensitive and empathic. People often misunderstand you and perceive an empathetic person as difficult. The empathic person can feel unaccepted because he or she is seen as different and has unique needs. Being empathic can seem like a limitation when it is a profound gift that, when harnessed, benefits all.

"Becoming more aware of your empathic nature and how you respond to fear will keep you focused in the present moment, which is where you access your inner power. You will discern the next best course of action that aligns with your highest purpose.

"On an individual level, self-doubt, fear, and a narrow view of life can restrict your ability to engage fully with our world and those in it.

"While you may understand my words intellectually, the mind cannot glean wisdom from experiences as the heart can. True wisdom, understanding, and compassion come from integrating your experiences into the heart."

I pause. With a long branch, I poke the fire, then pick up another piece of wood to toss on the coals. After a minute, flames wrap around the fresh fuel and grow bright.

"As you remember long-forgotten sacred mysteries, you will undergo shifts in consciousness that affect your behavior and outlook on life. Notate interesting and inspiring insights or observations in a journal. Later, when you look back, you can track the shifts in consciousness that document how much you have evolved.

"Join me if you are willing to remember your native abilities and talents, live closer to nature, create and exist with true equality in your relationships, and become free to follow your heart in occupations that fill you with vitality. I invite you to awaken and connect to your Divine nature. This journey is not for the faint of heart. However, the alternative of a shadow-dominated world is even less palatable. If we work together and honor our truth, we will prevail and protect Gea and her sister's worlds. There is not much time. We must act now. What does your spirit want?"

I settle on the log near the fire and slide the glowing embers together with the long branch. Murmurs from the women and men mingle with the tinkle of embers as they break apart. I wait tensely. I hope they will engage in this untested vision to heal our world. This is my experiment, and I want it to be a success. However, I will honor their choice.

A woman stands and shakes out her skirt. She glances at the others, who nod for her to continue.

"I speak for all of us. We are in. We want to stop the degradation of our world. Show us what we can do."

Releasing my pent breath, I smile. "Thank you."

I extract several sheets from the satchel that contains Cleric Paul's writings. "Let's start with a tale of how the Gea and the Droc'ri challenge came to be."

THE THREE SISTERS: A CREATION MYTH

In the beginning, the Great Mother Goddess birthed three daughters: Gea, Shara, and Earth. As a gift to her offspring, she swept her hand through the universe and pressed the dust she gathered into three spheres. She handed one to each of the young goddesses.

"Embrace these worlds as if they are you." As she spoke, three beautiful worlds took shape. She blessed each daughter and imprinted their essence into a world. The Great Mother said, "You are responsible for the life and well-being of all who live here as if it is your life and well-being. Care for these creations as you would your own children. You are the life of this creation that bears your beauty. Care for it as I have cared for you."

At first, the young goddesses marveled at the wondrous gifts from their mother. Placing the worlds next to each other, they spent eons admiring how each world reflected themselves and the Mother Goddess. The sisters watched the creatures in their own worlds, then compared what they saw in each other's. Their domains were beautiful and abundant, just as the sisters were beautiful and abundant. The Great Mother was pleased and praised each daughter for how well they tended their charges.

As the young goddesses matured, so too did their worlds. Imbued with subtle personality traits, each daughter engaged with and perceived life differently.

Willowy, sensitive Shara loved the water. She shaped her world into vast oceans and waterways that cut paths through her landmasses like gigantic canals. Shara loved the creatures that thrived in her waters. She spent days traveling through her world in an oyster-shell chariot pulled by six dolphins. Her watery steeds cavorted through the waves and inland passageways. Inspired to give her dolphins sport, Shara created many small, winding channels through continents. Soon, her world was filled with islands.

Not to be outdone by Shara, voluptuous, sensuous Earth created large continents and distributed them around her globe. Earth loved her dry lands and continually shaped the terrain like a potter molding clay. She squeezed together rocks and formed majestic, snow-covered mountains. In fertile valleys grew lush forests and expansive grasslands. She drew rivers with her fingernail. She brushed her fingertips across the treetops of her rain forests and ruffled the needles on her evergreen trees to smell the balsam aroma. Dressed in her finest silks and sampling fruity delights from her plant kingdom, Earth lounged on a mountaintop where she gloried in the world she had created.

After observing how Earth and Shara molded their worlds, elegant, wise Gea opted to keep an equilibrium between the elements in her world. As the balancer and peacemaker, she loved every creature and wanted them to live in harmony and find fulfillment. They were all valuable to her and played an essential role in making the world complete.

Gea's world seemed dull to her sisters, and they frequently chided her about it. In response, Gea would smile. She watched her sisters' friendly competition to gain the favor of their mother. Occasionally, she would suggest something one of them could try, or she would intervene in an argument. Unlike her sisters, who thought she was silly, she instilled Divine Magic into her world. This Magic went beyond the innate spirit that lived in everything. Gea not only wove an awareness of the Divine Mother into its tapestry but also provided a means for her inhabitants to access it easily when needed. She replied to her sisters' remarks with a gentle warning, "Though our worlds are thriving, it will not always be that way. Change is inevitable. One must prepare for the unforeseen."

Her mother's Divine Magic took root and permeated every life form, giving each beast, rock, and tree an awareness of their spirit.

Shara noticed. "I don't want the wisdom of the Great Mother lost. Since you already know how to do it, can you anchor the Great Mother's Magic into the fabric of my world, too?"

Gea agreed. "Earth, would you like to do the same?"

"Let me watch, and I can do what you do, Gea." However, eons passed, and Earth never imprinted her world as Gea had shown her. When Gea questioned her, Earth responded, "All my creations already have a soul. I don't need to do anything more."

As time passed, the continual reshaping by the sisters created distinct worlds that orbited each other on their journey around the sun. Shara and Earth became consumed with making their worlds more magnificent than the other, and their friendly competition turned into a rivalry.

One day, Earth rested on a mountaintop and gazed over her handiwork. The patchwork of green, brown, tan, and blue pleased her. More sensual and companionable than either of her siblings, Earth wished she had someone to share it with. She thought of Gea and Shara but shook her head. Shara's views of life were too deep and emotional. And Gea . . . well, Gea just wasn't exciting enough.

Lonely, Earth became saddened and wept. Her tears flooded her precious lands, eroding mountains and gouging deep gorges. She cried even more.

Gea came to her. "Sister, you must restore your heart. You are destroying your beautiful world."

Earth flung herself into her older sister's arms and cried, "I have no one with whom to share my beautiful domain. I have some of Shara's sea creatures but I want something special. Unique. I've been watching your new creatures—the two-legged ones. They are clever and could be more like us." She pleaded with her sister, "Share some of your human creations."

Gea gazed at Earth for a long time. "I would be happy to share the humans from my world with you, and I will also share them with Shara. We must maintain a balance to keep our planets stable. You will need to oversee your humans, for they will care for you as you care for them."

Earth nodded enthusiastically. "I'll watch over them. I'll do everything you tell me. When can I have them?"

Gea called Shara and Earth to her homeland. They sat at the top of the world and looked over Gea's lands and seas.

"Let me give you two pairs from each region. You must learn how to care for them before I give you more."

The sisters took their prizes back to their domains and placed them in the most hospitable environments. They watched over them like first-time mother hens over broods of chicks. Earth and Shara were ecstatic. The humans thrived, and their numbers grew.

Gea and the Great Mother were pleased and soon seeded more humans. For a time, Earth was delighted.

Gea and Shara were satisfied with the worlds given to them by the Great Mother. However, Earth wanted more. She watched her beasts mate and have offspring. She wanted to know what that felt like and wondered who the Great Mother's counterpart was. That was when she decided she wanted a mate who was her equal. Someone with whom she could create little Earths.

Then, one day, a stranger named Kurat arrived.

"I can make your home the loveliest paradise in the universe," he said with a winning smile. "Together, we will fashion more worlds like this one and rule the galaxy." His handsome features glowed with a golden light.

Earth admired his muscular form and imagined becoming a Great Mother of her own clutch of planets and stars. Yet, a tiny tickle inside warned Earth to be careful. She decided to test this charming god.

Kurat joined Earth in her chariot, pulled by four eagles. She found his presence intoxicating.

"What would you improve about my homeland?" she asked.

Kurat pointed at the two-legged ones. "These creatures can become the most powerful in your realm. Why do you keep them small?"

The question took Earth aback. "What do you mean? I love all my creations equally, and none is better than the other. Each plays a different role in my world, and I don't want to disturb the balance. It has been working perfectly for eons."

Kurat took Earth in his arms and kissed her. "And you have not been happy. I felt your plight from across the galaxy."

Earth had never felt the touch of a god such as this. She forgot about her creatures and surrendered to the seductive charms of this stranger from far away. Kurat entertained Earth with his many adventures across the galaxy. Lulled by his soothing voice, she fell into a deep sleep. Centuries passed. When she awoke, the stranger was gone. She searched everywhere, but there was no sign of Kurat. She noticed something was wrong. Instead of animals and humans mingling and foraging alongside each other, the humans clustered into groups and hunted their animal friends. And each other!

Earth was shocked. She transformed into a woman and walked her lands. She mingled with the animals in the forests and plains and listened to the trees and mountains. They all said the same thing. "Kurat has stolen the heart of our home and transformed it into his likeness. The males of the two-legged ones have claimed superiority. We are no longer safe. Please help us."

Earth changed into an eagle and spied upon the human camps. It was true. The males appeared to subjugate the females, mating brutally with their women as the urge drove them. They fought and killed each other. Their attitude toward the abundant land had turned possessive. Rather than find a peaceful resolution, they quickly resorted to violence. She abhorred violence and the despoiling of her realm.

Earth fled to Gea. She cried and cried. "What have I done? I have ruined my world. What can I do?"

Shara and Gea tried to console Earth.

"How could one god almost overnight destroy what has taken eons to build? I'll destroy my world and start over," she declared.

"Sister," Gea, the wise elder, said, "we are three facets of the One. If you demolish your realm, you will also shatter our domains and our connection. Instead, we will help you restore the balance. But the damage is done, and we must build on what remains. We cannot go in and cast out what has been seeded into the hearts of your inhabitants and the very heart of your world—your heart—without destroying you."

Gea put her arm around Earth. "You are precious, Sister. We will not let a jealous god's treachery undo your world. Instead, we will outsmart him. We must establish a way for your world to evolve and shift its frequency from what Kurat has entrained, yet make it look like he has succeeded. It will take time. We must let this cycle play out. Then you will have recovered your beautiful realm again."

Gea patted Earth on the shoulder. "It won't be easy. You must be strong and dedicated. And patient. We will aid you in this task."

They spent days resting in the Heartland Forest, listening to the ancient wisdom of the tree spirits. They formulated a plan.

"It's risky," Gea said. "If it doesn't work, we will cease to exist."

Shara added, "You must keep the Goddess alive in your world. Teach your people to live by listening to their hearts and remembering that they are not only united as a species but also one with all life forms in your world, ours, and the cosmos. If people forget they are all children of the Great Mother and lose their connection to Her, if magic is replaced by the intellect and the need for empirical proof, we will know we have failed."

Gea said, "Support the females of your population. Imprint on them the Great Mother's wisdom and the memory of the Goddess. Don't let them forget it. We must also merge our worlds into one planet. This will unite us so that Kurat cannot conquer us individually. He will have to deal with all three of us at once. And together, connected in this way, we can support you, Earth, and chase away the discord Kurat has sown."

"How do our worlds become one? Won't they all look alike?" Earth scowled at Shara, appalled at the thought of her world becoming a vast sea.

Gea smiled. "This is the best part. They will be stacked one on top of the other. Your world, Earth, will be innermost and the most protected. Shara will be in the middle. My world will be the most exposed. With the Great Mother's help, I will place a shield around our planet and add two moons to watch over our worlds and deceive Kurat." She handed Earth and Shara each a basket of crystals. "Plant these around your realms. They connect our separate domains and will help to amplify the Mother Goddess's Divine Love in yours. Protect these crystals. They are your lifeline to the Mother and are critical to our survival."

Earth was still uncertain.

"Our planets will merge and occupy the same space." Gea continued to explain, "However, our individual worlds will be separated by a veil of energy. To your inhabitants, nothing has changed."

Shara nodded. "Clever, Gea."

Heartened, Earth returned home, determined to undo the damage caused by her lover's betrayal. Transforming into a wise woman, she journeyed from clan to clan. She chose a woman from each village, imprinted her with the wisdom of the Great Mother, and declared her the leader of her people. Each priestess received a blessing for protection against the male forces aligned with Kurat, who sought to depose her.

Earth instructed her priestesses to build sacred schools to teach the mysteries of the Great Mother Goddess. She changed women's brain structure so women would always have a connection to the Goddess, no matter what they had to endure. This wisdom would pass down through the maternal line. Over many generations of men incarnating into female bodies and receiving the essence of the Goddess, the cold-hearted ambitions that Kurat had implanted into the males of the human species would be tamed.

Following Gea's guidance, Earth dictated one Divine Truth to her priestesses.

"Everyone—every human, animal, plant, rock, tree, everything seen and unseen—all of us are children of the Great Mother and are alive with Her Spirit. We are Divine expressions of her. The same force—the Great Mother—animates everything. All creations serve and are equal in the eyes of the Mother, and all are sovereign. Even the rocks and trees are free to choose their life path. Remember this above all else, and let it be your guide."

Earth watched over her humans. She wept at how her women were treated as she perceived Kurat had treated her—taking her world that wasn't his to take, degrading the respect and equality between life forms, and instead, transforming her human women into lowly servants and property to be bartered for what could be gained. Whether using charm or force, it had the same result.

Earth withdrew to her mountaintop. She didn't want to watch anymore. When her sadness made her weep, the world flooded. Other times she became angry, and massive storms swept across the lands and seas, destroying anything in their wake. She felt life being sucked from her. She begged her sisters for help.

Gea came to where she lay, cradled in an enormous volcano. Steam rose around her, and the mountain rumbled ominously.

"I'm trying to be patient, Sister," Earth said. "I get angry at what Kurat did to me and my world, and I am angry at my human populations, who rape and pillage my women and me without considering the consequences or the harm they are doing. Instead of finding peaceful solutions, they bicker and fight over resources, believing they don't have enough. They have brought the world to the brink of annihilation several times with their weapons and senseless disregard for the dangerous substances they meddle with. They poison me and my living things."

Earth sighed. Stretching out her arm, she jabbed the earth, and it shook. "Magic is lost," she said quietly. A flower becomes a combination of petals, stamen, and chemicals. Forgotten are the flower's essence and acknowledgment of the transformative effects of a flower's beauty on one's psyche, the calming or stimulating effects of her scent, and color frequencies that merge mind and heart.

"All but a few outcasts have forgotten the Great Mother. My priestesses have almost been destroyed, replaced by male-dominated organizations claiming to be the spokesman for the Divine. These organizations serve as another way to control people through fear. There is only a handful of my lineage that remember. Sadly, my beautiful and abundant realm has become a wasteland and the playground for Kurat's Dark Lords." Earth sighed again. "Sometimes, I feel like igniting all the volcanoes and ending the two-legged ones."

Gea sat beside her sister and put an arm around her shoulders. "I know, Earth. This scourge of unconsciousness, aided by Kurat's Dark Lord minions, has also invaded Shara's world and mine. Kurat . . ." Gea hesitated.

"What is it, Gea?"

"Not long after he came to you, Kurat visited Shara's world."

Earth sat up abruptly. The land beneath her rumbled. "What has he done to Shara?"

Disguised as an albatross, he approached her while she rested on an island and watched her dolphins play. He tried to woo her, but she saw through his illusion. He came back again, this time as a salmon. Not knowing his true nature, one of her servants brought him to her on a platter. She was about to eat him when one of her dolphins leaped onto the table and consumed him. The dolphin died immediately. Aggrieved, Shara cast Kurat out, forbidding him from returning.

"When stony-hearted Kurat enchanted you, you didn't know he had allied with the Dark Lords. In retaliation for Shara's rejection, he ordered his servants, the Lizard clans, to invade her world. The clans act like locusts, swarming from planet to planet, breeding, and consuming all life and resources to raise their offspring. Kurat and his Lizard clan allies plan to overthrow the Great Mother and become the Master of the universes." Gea patted Earth's arm. "Don't feel bad, Sister. He is a master of deceit. That's why you didn't recognize him for who he was. He has raped many a realm, leaving his mark upon the few that have survived. He takes by force what he couldn't claim with charm as he did you." Gea shuddered. "Evil creature. Even if he is a child of the Great Mother and our older brother."

"Why does he challenge our Mother? What can we do?"

"Kurat was created to sow chaos in the universes. He causes us to become creative. By working together, we can outsmart him and survive. I have an idea." Gea started humming a melody. "Do you remember Mother singing this to us when we were young?" Earth nodded. "It is her creation song. We can use it to make our worlds whole again. Let's get Shara and sing it together and recreate our worlds."

Earth made space for Gea to settle beside her, and the two goddesses started singing. Soon Shara joined them, and they sang for centuries.

Earth relaxed. Before her, she noticed subtle shifts in the terrain and felt subtle awakenings in her body. She smiled.

"My priestesses, the Spirit Women of Shara, and the Gra'Bandia Healers awaken. Kurat's influence is harnessed now. We shall prevail, Sisters. Thank you."

Placing the sheets of parchment with the rest of the document, I settle onto my log by the fire and watch.

One woman asks, "Is Cleric Paul suggesting that the worlds of Earth, Shara, and Gea are interconnected by an invisible, shared planetary matrix and are linked by the crystals each sister embedded into their world? I've seen those crystals sometimes in my dreams."

"So have I," another woman says. "I've had glimpses of foreign worlds that feel like they are part of ours."

"How can we help them? We can't see them or go there," another asks.

"The taint that invades and threatens to destroy our world is strongest in Earth's realm. While we can't physically go there to aid in uplifting her world, we can, through our actions here in Gea, transmit the Mother Goddess's Love and Light to her worlds. In so doing, we support Gea's sisters in their struggles. By assisting Earth and Shara, we strengthen the Goddess's presence in Gea and can cast out the dark threat."

"This seems pretty daunting, even impossible," the pair'ti of the last speaker says.

"It does seem impossible." I take a deep breath and exhale slowly. "Yet, we must try. It is important we understand what is at stake. According to Cleric Paul's interpretations, Gea is the only world that can keep the three sisters united. There is an ancient prophecy foretelling the fall of the three sisters unless certain conditions can be met. The foretelling warns of a time when the forces of chaos will outweigh the power of peace in the world's heart and all its inhabitants. Unless balance within each world is restored and harmony established within and between our worlds, our planet, and all three coexisting worlds, will be annihilated.

"What we do will affect our two sister worlds just as they affect us. The stakes are high. Our very existence and billions of lives—some aware but most not—will cease to exist, and the Goddess will lose valuable allies in the Cosmic rebalancing. Though the task seems beyond our comprehension, we must try. We must succeed."

"Then let's get started," a woman to my left says.

"Let's start on the path of self-understanding with the story of Cat and Dog."

REMEMBERING YOUR TRUE NATURE

Cat and Dog

Cat and Dog met under an old maple tree, whose long limbs offered a refreshing respite from the scorching sun. Cat lay on the ground, stretching her legs. Dog hunkered down, keeping a respectful distance from her after having felt the claws of her displeasure more often than he liked.

Cat watched him through half-closed eyes. The corners of her lips turned upward. *I'm the queen here*, she thought, *as it should be*. She repositioned herself, ensuring Dog would notice the slight twitch of her tail. She enjoyed provoking Dog.

Dog tried to ignore her. He lay his chin on his paws and pretended to sleep, but his slightly cocked ears gave him away. He would have put more distance between himself and his nemesis, but this was the best spot under the tree. *No. Cat has the coolest place*, he thought, sighing. He knew better than to challenge Cat.

A while later, their mistress joined them under the tree. Cat lifted her head and stared at Dog.

"Mistress is mine," she said.

Not to be outdone, Dog said, "Mistress is part of my pack. You don't have a pack. I do."

Cat stretched, flexing her claws.

Dog continued, "I serve Mistress. I watch over her and protect her. I am her loyal companion."

Cat yawned widely, showing sharp fangs. Though she said nothing, the tip of her tail twitched. Finally, Cat said, "I show Mistress how to be independent and self-sufficient, something you can't do, Dog. I show her how never to settle for less than she deserves, never to deny who she is. You," she twitched an ear, "do somersaults to please Mistress."

Dog scooted closer to his person. "Mistress loves me, and I love her."

Cat half-closed her eyes. "How little you know, Dog. Just because you are her companion and you serve her every whim doesn't mean she loves you more than she loves me."

"How can you say that?" Dog growled.

Cat stood and arched her back. With calculated grace, she stretched one hind leg behind her, then the other. She repositioned herself on the opposite side of Mistress. She lay down with her head on Mistress's thigh. Dog placed his muzzle on her other leg. Nose to nose, the two animals stared at each other.

Cat said, "You don't believe me, do you? Let's put this to the test. I'll prove she loves me more than you."

The two animals walked a short distance away. Cat told Dog, "Do what you think will win the love of Mistress, and I will do what I think I need to do."

Dog ran off, searching the garden for something he could bring back that would please Mistress. In the meantime, Cat returned to Mistress, climbed onto her lap, and purred. Automatically, Mistress looked down and petted the furry creature, who purred even more.

When Dog returned with a bone, he dropped it before Mistress and stared at Cat, who lifted her head slightly to give him a superior look.

"You're in my spot," Dog barked.

Cat purred louder. Dog barked again.

"Leave Cat alone. If you can't be polite, go somewhere else," Mistress scolded.

Dog went a few feet away and lay down with his head on his paws, watching Cat bask in Mistress's attention.

She'll pay for tricking me, he growled. *I'll wait until she is preoccupied and alone and then chase her.* He imagined chasing Cat around the garden.

Mistress patted the ground beside her, inviting Dog to lie beside her. He jumped up and made a display of finding just the right place. The grim line of his mouth softened.

"Mistress does love me," he murmured to Cat.

Cat ignored him and purred louder.

Dog sighed. *Cat treats Mistress as her servant. I don't do that. I love Mistress, no matter what she does. And she loves me... And she loves Cat, too.*

Cat smiled. Once again, she had made her point. "That's the beauty, Dog. You serve Mistress. Mistress serves me." She shifted to let a leg dangle off Mistress's lap near the dog and closed her eyes.

The Healer's Path: Ellara's Wisdom

Remembering Your True Nature

The first steps on the Healer's path are to become acquainted with who you are.

As the story of Cat and Dog suggests, each of us is born with a particular set of gifts and abilities. Some people have natural charisma and can attract and lead people. Others are conscientious craftspeople or visionaries and healers. These talents act like guiding forces for the roles we play with our families, in our communities, and in the world. Let's use Cat and Dog to illustrate this.

If you've ever watched a dog and a cat for any length of time, you will have noticed that each animal has a distinct way it approaches life. Dogs want to serve and be our friends. They are loyal, and dependable, and provide us with an accurate reflection of ourselves.

On the other hand, cats act as if we are their servants. They are more aloof and independent than most dogs. A cat would never deign to be a dog. It is absolutely beneath her dignity to be anything but who she is. She reminds us to remember who we are.

Like Cat and Dog, we wear a personality and set of behaviors that dictate how we interact with others; this is how others easily identify us.

When Nana first mentored me, she made me practice feeling what it was like to be a cat, a dog, a squirrel, or a tree. She would say, "You can't know anything until you become it."

I'd stare at her in silent resistance, but she would point with her cane. Fearing her disapproval, I'd comply. The first few times, it was awkward. Then it became fun. And Nana was right. I learned far more from merging with the animal or tree than I could from Cleric Paul's books.

One day she asked, "You have been a rock, a bird, a tree, a cat, a deer. What do they all have in common?" Wondering what she wanted to hear, I shrugged. "They are all alive."

She thumped her cane on the ground. "What if I were to suggest you, I, and all that you see are Goddess-born? She lives within each thing. Her Radiance, Her Love animates, and gives life to everything." She tilted her head to one side and peered at me like a chicken when looking for a bug.

"Let me share a Divine Truth," she continued, satisfied by my puzzlement. "No matter your gender, what you look like, whether you are a rock, tree or animal, you are the Goddess. You carry Her divine nature within."

"But..." I started.

"This is a tough concept to grasp. We start by seeing the Goddess as outside ourselves. We petition Her to help us, to make the crops grow for abundant harvests, and to heal another for us. But the truth is, all the power of the Goddess is within each of us, just waiting to be tapped. You are the one who does the healing, who makes the crops abundant, who helps another. Through being who we are, we connect with and feel her Radiance, her Love."

She tapped my chest with her cane. "Child, this requires a complete acceptance of yourself and surrendering of Ego, which the Goddess created as a gift to protect you and keep you safe from danger. The very nature of the Ego is geared toward your physical survival. It motivates you to find food, shelter, and a companion. The Droc'ri sorcerers and other dark organizations mainly focus on primal needs and often struggle to have these needs met. They have closed their hearts to the magic and beauty of the Goddess. They strive for more and are never satisfied because they believe they must obtain everything on their own. It takes surrendering to the Divine to find meaning and fulfillment in life. With patience and care, you can accept the Divine within and be guided to your highest purpose."

Nana walked to the area behind her house. She pointed to where water pooled in the creek. "What do you see?"

"Grass and wild plants line the creek. Colored rocks cover the bottom of the creek. Several water flowers and the reflection of the sky and trees."

Nana grunted. I suspected this was not the answer she expected.

She continued, "Like images reflected in a pool, we are reflections of the Goddess. And like the Goddess, the greater part of us remains invisible and lives in the nonphysical realms. All life forms are complex, multi-dimensional beings."

I have since learned the wisdom and the inherent power that is in all of us once we understand the full meaning of being Goddess-born and child of the Goddess. All creation is a child of the Goddess.

Applying Ellara's Wisdom

Remembering Your True Nature Practices

1: Calming the Mind

The first step to understanding your true nature is to calm the mind. A straightforward method is through a breathing exercise. This breathing practice can be used anywhere and at any time. It is the foundation for the practices in this workbook. It creates empty spaces in your thoughts, plants your feet firmly on the ground, and raises your awareness about your body, anchoring you in the present moment.

Calming the Mind with Breathwork

Stand, sit, or lie down. Closing your eyes may make this practice easier.

Place your hands lightly over your heart. Deeply inhale to the count of four heartbeats.

Exhale slowly to the count of six or eight heartbeats.

After inhaling, pause for a few seconds before exhaling. Then pause before taking another breath. The pause stills the mind.

Keep breathing in this way and notice how your breath affects your body.

As you inhale, feel how your body physically responds to your breathing and how the ground supports you.

As you exhale, take note of the same physical sensations and if they differ. Notice how your chest and abdomen move. Do you feel lighter when you inhale and heavier when you exhale?

Allow your awareness to expand so that you settle more deeply into the earth when you exhale and release tension in your body. Imagine a strong cord running from the base of your spine, deep into the earth, tethering you to a golden ring in the core.

Continue with slow, deep breaths. Don't cling to any thoughts. Let the mind calm. This allows you to sense the subtle forces you receive from the environment, such as sensations in your body. You may also see images with your inner sight or hear messages from your spirit team. Each time thoughts distract you, bring your attention back to your breath and the support of the ground.

Now, place your attention on your heart and inhale, imagining your breath going into, around, and behind your heart.

Notice your heart relax, open, and expand. If you find this difficult, tap your chest over your heart several times. Or find something to be grateful for. An expanded heart can feel like you have dissolved into the surrounding space. Your aura is vast. Or it can feel like you are wrapped in a warm, soft blanket. Continue to breathe slowly and regularly. Don't let your mind participate.

Listen with your body. Hear or see with your inner sight.

Notice how your body feels and what you receive. Notice what you feel or sense in the space around you. You may feel a slight air movement or smell the sweet scent of roses or lemon blossoms. Perhaps you hear bird songs, travelers passing by, or the wind in the trees. Notice the level of tension in your body, how primary energy centers—such as your solar plexus, heart, and throat—feel, and notice your emotional state.

This is a basic breathwork practice. Five to fifteen minutes performed regularly will yield results. The goal is to slow the cascade of thoughts and spend more time paying attention to what is happening around you in the moment.

Try this practice now for five or ten minutes.

What did you notice? Did you have a steady stream of thoughts? What was the nature of those thoughts? Were they fixed on one topic, person, or situation?

Were you able to slow them down by paying attention to your breathing? Did counting the duration of the inhales and exhales distract your mind?

What did you notice in your body?

Calming the mind is something that takes time and persistent practice. Don't judge yourself if your mind refuses to become tamed. Just notice, without judging or self-criticizing.

Calming the Mind with Bergamot Essential Oil.

While breathing, hold a drop of oil of bergamot on the point known as the "spirit gate point" or Shen Men ear point. Hold the top of your ear closest to your face with your thumb and forefinger. Your thumb will naturally fall into the indent on the inside fold of the ear. This point works to calm and balance the mind.

Calming the Mind with Gratitude

Another trick to slow racing thoughts is to notice them without getting trapped by them. When you fret over something, breathe and thank your mind for those thoughts. Acknowledge how important they are to you. Appreciate your powerful mind and thank it for working so hard.

Calming the Mind by Noticing

If that doesn't work, focus on something in your immediate environment, such as a plant, a table, or a stone. Notice every detail about it. Alternatively, you could listen to identify the subtle sounds around you. This takes you out of your head and into the here and now.

Some people are designed to have more active minds. They relate to the world through their minds. Their keen ability to analyze and strategize is a powerful part of their character. If this is you, taming your mind is like trying to put a recalcitrant horse into a harness. It can be done with sufficient determination. Be gentle with yourself.

As you develop this simple practice, you can apply it to any situation. Once you have trained your body and mind to calm by repeating this ritual, you can collect yourself and regain a sense of composure in just a few breaths. It doesn't mean the problem has gone away. You have more of your wits about you to decide what to do.

Take this practice into your daily life by noticing yourself in various situations. Calming breath work is useful for introverted or empathic people when facing social events or challenging situations.

Spend time alone. Quality alone time means active awareness of yourself and of your body while you engage in solitary activities. This could be meditation, walks in nature, cooking, household chores, working on a craft that nurtures you, writing, bathing, or many activities you do alone. Notice your thoughts when you are alone, without judgment or analyzing what they mean. In time, your body becomes a guide to teach you the meanings of what you receive. This takes practice and open-mindedness. Simply be present.

2: CONNECTING TO THE DIVINE

Your natural senses take over once you tame your mind and spend more time in the present. You become more aware of your environment. Your senses reach beyond the material world and into the realms of spirit. We are multi-dimensional beings, and seeing beyond the ordinary is part of our heritage. Let's practice with your enhanced senses.

Go for a walk outside in nature and feel the space around you. Focus on your body or an object in front of you as you inhale. Then let your awareness expand as you exhale as if you are viewing the world through energetic peripheral vision.

Do you notice the plants, the herbs, the flowers, and the trees? Or hear the birds sing? Feel the sun on your back and face?

This is the Divine in Her many expressions.

What happens when you expand your mind and your inner vision to see the energies surrounding you?

Allow the grasses, the trees, and the animals to speak to you.

Do you sense more with your body, hear voices, or receive impressions or see images?

Make a daily practice of engaging with the world with your heightened senses. Your life becomes richer.

3: Expanding Your Awareness

Make a sanctuary in your home where you can be alone and at peace.

Light a candle and allow yourself to be mesmerized by the flame. As you breathe, let your awareness expand and connect with everything around you.

Let your imagination wander to the objects before you.

Let your awareness expand.

What do you hear?

What do you smell?

What do you feel?

What thoughts wander into your mind?

Bring your awareness back to your breath and your breath's effect on your body.

Finish the practice by blowing out the candle.

THE BENEFITS OF SELF-REFLECTION

To live an aware life is to develop a habit of self-reflection. These are questions you ask yourself anytime, particularly when you are stressed or anxious about a situation or event.

It has been my experience that when I understand why I react a certain way, then I can decide whether I want to continue along this energetic path or change it. Usually, I want to change it.

Sometimes I don't want to know and live in denial for a while. However, I have learned that my spirit is incredibly patient and persistent, so if I ignore one opportunity to learn something about myself, my behaviors, and my relationship with life, I will get another opportunity and another until I finally pay attention.
How often have you come up against a recurring event?

You say, "I've already been through this. Why has it come back?"

Self-reflection builds a relationship with yourself, your inner knowing, and your spiritual self. Be mindful of what drives you and the opportunities life presents. Reclaim your power to choose. Wise choices require insightful information.

You're invited to be curious, to see outside the box, and see from another, broader perspective.
What else could be true?
Is there a different way I could perceive this person or situation?
Where can I be more compassionate?

What do I want? What does my spirit want?

What happens if I do or don't ask for what I want?

What's at stake?

These are just some general questions to keep in the back of your mind as you go through life.

The chapter's self-reflection prompts relate to the theme of the teaching. You're invited to delve deep into your answers, even if it is scary. No one will see these but you.

Take as long as you need with each question. You can do one question a day or several. You can breeze through them, get an overview, then come back for a more in-depth exploration.

Do not limit yourself to these questions. Allow and trust your inner guidance to lead you to the insights and wisdom you need currently and guide you to your next best step. What you answer now is perfect.

Write your comments and responses in a journal. You find that when you come back later, in six months, a year, or several years, some of your responses will be similar, and others will be different. This is the inherent magic of the adventure you are on. Enjoy the process.

SELF-REFLECTION PROMPTS

Do you resonate more with a cat or a dog? Or another animal?

What attributes of the animal do you relate to?

Are you the one who serves, or are you the one who is served?

Do you feel selfish (or guilty) when others do things for you?

When do you feel taken advantage of?

What distinctive traits do you have? It might be a particular way you do things, certain foods you favor, or patterns of thinking.

Do you see your unique talents as friendly support for you?

Have there been times in your life when you have felt judged and unworthy because you didn't fit in or had different interests or appearance than others?

Do the people in your life accept you and respect your natural abilities, or are (were) you required to live according to their expectations?

What were others' expectations of you?

What did you sacrifice to fit in?

What effect did it have on your life?

Do you feel a connection with the Divine?

Can you see yourself as a reflection of the Divine?

Can you recognize you are part of the same human family, the Earth family? You have the same basic needs as everyone, everything else. Yet you are unique in that you express a particular pattern of frequencies that distinguishes you from others. This means you meet your basic needs in your own unique style.

What can you change to strengthen your understanding that we are all connected?

How would that show up in your daily life?

Can you see how our world supports you in every way?

Can you see how you are more powerful than you think?

What small step can you take today to live one of your gifts fully?

In the following sections, we will look at several obstacles that distract you from your purpose: fear, self-doubt, and feelings of unworthiness. You will explore these concepts for yourself and observe how they apply to or affect your life.

Some of these elements have deep roots in your energy field and may extend into other lifetimes.

Self-limiting attitudes start in childhood and can be amplified as we get older.

Our ancestors may also pass them down to us.

To overcome these challenges, you must find the courage to face them, acknowledge them, and accept that they have served a purpose, often of keeping you safe and protected.

These beliefs about yourself can also paralyze you, restrict you from reclaiming your inner power, and hamper your determination to overcome the shadows you face. They keep you small, submissive, and prey to be controlled by others.

Letting go of old beliefs about yourself makes room for new awareness about your power.

In the next story, notice how Wolf Pup must overcome his doubts.

TAMING SELF-DOUBT

The Wolf Pup and the Raging Stream

Wolf's family paused at the edge of a raging stream. Scouting ahead, Wolf Father yipped, "We can cross here."

A tall tree had fallen across the cascading water, forming a bridge to the other side. Boldly, Wolf Father stepped onto the smooth bark of the slender tree and trotted across.

"Come on," he called to the others. He sniffed the air while he waited for his family to cross.

The young wolves trotted across with no difficulty. Then came the time for the new pups. Wolf Mother nudged them and, one-by-one, they climbed onto the log and tottered across.

One pup remained. He eyed the water apprehensively. His mother touched him with her nose.

"I can't," he whined. "I don't want to fall in, like my brother did a few weeks ago, and get washed away." He pushed against his mother. "Carry me across as you did before."

"I can't, Son. You're too big now." She looked to his brothers and sisters. "They went across without incident. You can, too." She butted his rump with her muzzle to move him forward.

He climbed onto the tree trunk, where it rested firmly on the bank. The tree was not wide, and he would have to walk carefully.

"Go ahead. I'll be right behind you."

The young wolf pup took a step and slipped on a loose piece of bark, almost losing his balance. He jumped back to solid ground. "I can't," he whined again.

"Come on. Wolf Father has moved on. We need to catch up."

The pup lay down. "I'll fall in and be swallowed by the water."

Wolf Mother watched the rest of her family recede into the distance. She sat down beside her son.

"I was very sad to lose your brother to the water spirits. I don't want that same fate for you. You practiced in the creek at our old home until you became an excellent swimmer. You even said you liked water."

The pup put his chin on the earth between his paws. "I know. But this is different. I was never good at walking on trees. And this creek is too fast."

"You easily walked along the brink of the gulch by our old home. That required precise placement of your feet. This is no different. Think of this as walking on the edge and remember how much you like water."

Wolf Mother waited. Finally, the pup stood up.

"Alright. Can I hold on to your tail, just in case?"

Returning to the tree trunk, he climbed up behind his mother. With her tail in his teeth, he took one step at a time and crossed to the other side. He jumped off the upper limbs of the fallen tree and bounced happily around his mother. She licked his face.

"I'm proud of you, Son. Let the memory of this accomplishment give you the courage to try something beyond what you think you can do. Now, let's catch up with the rest of our family."

The Healer's Path: Ellara's Wisdom

Taming Self-Doubt

Like the wolf pup, to gain any proficiency in my talent and to create the intimate connection I enjoyed with my beloved mate, Sam, I had to first overcome self-doubt and feelings of unworthiness. Often, the seeds of mistrust start in response to childhood events.

My childhood didn't foster self-trust or self-value. We had a small sheep and horse ranch far from Sheldon, and few visitors came. My mother thrust me into feeding and tending our animals, weeding the garden, and cleaning the wool. The memory of the hours spent carding and spinning yarn still makes me shudder. Often, I escaped into a world of my making. They frowned upon me doing things I could easily do, such as calming the herd during a storm or helping an animal with birthing.

My mother's infirmity, however, was a blessing. It allowed me the freedom to follow my childhood whims unsupervised. Yet, I was afraid of Nana Magog. She scowled at me when Trevor, my step-father, told stories of how, when I was very young, I had healed a mare who had a difficult birthing or any of my other toddler antics. Hearing these stories of me as a child caused me to question my judgment. Though I tended the animals growing up, I couldn't do what Trevor said I had done as a three-year-old. I doubted myself. I didn't believe I had any gifts because I didn't have Nana's magic or proficiency at weaving.

Even though I grew up in a society that valued women, I had to learn to respect and value myself before anyone could value me. I couldn't pop in and out of our home, light the fire, or restore someone to health as Nana did. However, talking with the animals came easily. So did seeing things that weren't visible to others and feeling sudden pains in my body when a visitor or Sam came. Of course, my inquiries were met with stony silence. I learned about these mysteries on my own.

As a sea captain, Sam traveled across the water to the mainland. He was my window into the outside world. He secretly brought me books about magic and healing and told me stories of his travels. I loved it when he came to visit. Good-naturedly, he let me try some of the healing techniques from the books on him, and bit by bit, I could make sense of what I read. Judging by my mother's wariness and Nana's curt comments, I suspected they disapproved of Sam.

The more I saw I had a gift and valued myself for it, the stronger the gift became and the more proficient I grew at healing. It was an arduous process. Despite what others said, I had to start small and listen to my inner guidance.

The catalyst that started me on my path was healing Sam of his injury so we could become hand-fasted. I recount my story in *The Rebel Healers*. But I didn't include in the story the internal struggle I had to deal with and the dark forces that Nana's training awoke.

It started after I returned home the first night after my attempt to restore Sam. Sam had departed for another run to Langon. I lay in my bed, my mind mulling over the day and my frustration at not accomplishing what Nana expected of me. I must have drifted off.

Suddenly, I awoke, gasping for air. Invisible hands clutched my throat, suppressing any ability to cry for help. With fingers clawing at the ephemeral hands around my throat, I struggled to sit up. Woven into the darkness around me was a black creature. It wrapped me in a clammy embrace. Tendrils stabbed into my body and found a home in my heart, solar plexus, and womb. Into my mind came the words, "You belong to me. No one will have you. If you continue this training, you and anyone you touch will die." I sensed the menace in its words and was terrified. As suddenly as it came, it was gone.

Wide-eyed and peering into the darkness, I didn't sleep for the rest of the night. I resolved I would never become a Healer.

Making up excuses, I refused to go to Nana's the following days. My mother eyed me with a strange expression but said nothing. She didn't object to the halt in my training. She hadn't approved.

When Sam returned after two weeks, and I told him I couldn't finish restoring him because of a black creature that was in my body, he nodded slowly. He placed a hand lightly on my shoulder and said, "The black creature does not become part of you unless you allow it. You have the gift, but it is your choice if you want to master it."

I started crying. By denying him healing, he would live the rest of his life in pain, and we could never be together in the way we wanted. My mother would be pleased. "I don't know how to deal with the darkness within me. I want to heal you but don't want to transmit this evil creature to you."

Sam held me for a long while. Finally, he said. "Do what feels right. I support you in whatever you choose." Then he held me at arm's length and grinned. "It's a shame to waste your talent, though."

With Sam's encouragement, I continued my training with Nana. I discovered that when I brought the Goddess's Divine Love and Light into my being, it chased away my fears and, bit by bit, dissolved the darkness. I am still watchful for the dark beast that lives within, and whenever something goes wrong, I'm quick to think it's my fault. You can tame doubts, but the seeds of doubt are always ready to resurface when you need to be courageous.

When you have lived in self-doubt and unworthiness your whole life, it sounds selfish to tell people of your successes or to acknowledge your talents. It is hard to speak up or make choices about what you want. It's a lot easier to let someone else decide for you. The only problem is that their choices work for them and may or may not work for you. And if you try to decide on your own, someone is always ready to tell you why it won't work or that it's the wrong choice.

Taming the self-doubt creature takes dedication and shifting your perception of yourself. It requires acknowledging your accomplishments.

Healing Self-Doubt with Trust

The opposite of self-doubt is self-trust. How easy or hard is it for you to trust yourself and others? What does trust mean to you? Does trust equal "risk"?

Interestingly, the vibration of some names or birth dates fosters the energy of trust. I don't have the trust number in my name or birth date. I've struggled to trust myself and others. It takes time for me to let someone into my inner sphere.

If you wonder how trusting you are, try sharing a secret about yourself—something very intimate that you'd never tell a soul—with your partner. Could you do it? How did that feel?

Even though the Alban Society is built on trust—trust in the Goddess that all would be provided as it was needed, trust in each other, and trust in business dealings—I never felt like I could totally trust anyone, including the Goddess, during my younger years. Perhaps my mother and Nana Magog engendered this reluctance through the subtle undercurrents of mistrust they displayed. My mother didn't like visitors coming to our house, and when any buyers for our animals came, she made me stay beside her. Unspeaking, she watched the tradesmen until they left. She was skeptical of any invitations to go to Sheldon as well. As a young child, I didn't understand why she was so suspicious or protective. As a child does, I took on my mother's quirks without understanding her reasoning.

As a result, I became wary of the people I encountered. All except for Sam. He felt familiar.

I trusted those close to me, except Nana Magog. As a youngster, I couldn't make sense of her. She was stern and spoke harshly to my mother. I was afraid of her. When one is afraid, one can't trust.

When Nana started showing me simple healing methods, she told me I had to trust.

She would say, "Surrender to the Goddess and let her work through you. If you want to heal Sam from his injury, you must surrender and open your heart to the Goddess."

My treatments were significantly more effective after learning how to release the armor around my heart.

Cleric Paul said, "Our survival instinct is oriented to remembering all the times we have been betrayed, abandoned, hurt by someone, or felt abandoned by the Goddess. Each of us carries our mothers' and grandmother's fears, hurts, and pains."

This lack of trust made it hard to fully surrender to the Goddess so I could do my healing work. Trust meant becoming vulnerable. It has taken me years to trust that the Goddess will protect me. I am still watchful of strangers, mainly since I am hunted for my talent and what I represent, but I have learned that not every stranger means harm.

Mistrust is another face of fear: fear of being betrayed, abandoned, or hurt. Seeing the world and its inhabitants as dangerous sets the stage for ill fortune to befall us. I had to shift my mistrust into caution and discernment. I had to see myself as resilient and capable of handling adversity. Luckily, I learned how to read a person's energy before I engaged with them. I often remind myself that even though someone may or may not be behaving supportively, he is still a child of the Goddess, and we are more alike than not.

Trust is an invisible energy. You can say, "I trust you," or, "I don't trust you." What does that really mean? It takes courage to trust. After all, what if you're wrong and make a mistake?

Trust is an inner knowing, a certainty that your choice will be right. Even if it turns out disastrously, trust there is a hidden blessing. Trust is a state of being that must be cultivated, as you would tend the most precious flowers in your garden. Like flowers, trust requires watering—reminding yourself of how the past has worked out well. In time, the more trust has paid off, the easier it is to trust.

APPLYING ELLARA'S WISDOM

Developing Trust Daily Practices

For these practices, you will need your journal, and essential oils of rose, and jasmine. You can substitute rose hydrosol or rose lotion. Make sure the oils and cream are pure.

4: GRATITUDE DAILY PRACTICE

Here is a simple exercise to appreciate yourself.

Write the following in your journal:

Five things you like or appreciate about yourself.

Five things you are grateful for.

Five things you accomplished today.

Notice the small things, such as having a warm bed to sleep in, what you had to eat, how you got dressed, or whether you took the dog for a walk. It's the little things that add up and accumulate. Do this daily for at least three weeks. Notice any shifts in how you feel about yourself.

 ## 5: PRACTICING SELF-LOVE

How we feel about ourselves sets the tone for how we see the world and our place in it. We lose our inner strength without a healthy respect and appreciation for ourselves. We succumb to feelings of self-doubt, unworthiness, and fear. I've found this practice to be a powerful antidote for any of the self-imposed limitations we place on ourselves.

Self-Love Practice With Rose Essential Oil

Take a drop of oil of rose and place it on the tip of your little finger. Share the drop with the corresponding fingertip on the other hand. Touch and hold your fingertips over your heart. This practice is most effective if you face yourself in a mirror.

Say the following (or use your own words):

"Thank you, Rose, for sharing your Divine Gifts with me. I receive the Divine Gifts of rose into my being with love, gratitude, and appreciation.

"Thank you, Rose, for bringing Divine Love into my being, cradling each cell in my body in a matrix of Divine Love. Filling each and every cell with Divine Love so I become Divine Love and radiate Divine Love into the world, awakening Divine Love in others.

"I am Divine Love. Divine Love is me.

"I love myself. I trust myself. I am worthy.

"I accept myself. I appreciate myself. I am valuable.

"I adore myself. I respect myself. I deserve.

"I forgive myself. I forgive others. I am precious.

"I am beautiful. I am powerful. I am wise.

"Thank you. All is well."

Repeat this practice daily for at least three weeks.

A variation of this practice is to place your hands on your heart and breathe. Say: "From the depths of my heart, I love, accept and appreciate myself." Repeat this until you feel your heart expand or you feel warmth embracing you.

6: Building Self-Trust

Building self-trust is a gradual process that cannot be accomplished overnight. When someone says one thing and does another or promises to take an action, such as to pay a bill or quit smoking and they don't, a distrust develops for that person. It may be low level, or it could be prominent. The same distrust can develop in how we perceive ourselves.

Our experiences in the external world mirror the level of self-trust we possess. What irritates us most about another person is often a place where we have not been honest with ourselves.

What do you tell yourself? Does the little critical voice in your head say things like, "You don't make good decisions?" "You're not good with money?" "You'll never find that special someone?"

Trust wounds can cut deep and often originate in childhood or from our ancestors. Feeling betrayed by your parents or feeling abandoned by the Divine is another. Add a little unhealthy shame, and you have the perfect storm for lack of self-trust. Sometimes lack of trust and its sources are handed down through the generations, like an ancestral curse.

No matter the source, trust can be rebuilt with practice and reinforcing your self-talk with the times you dared to trust, which paid off.

Here is a healing practice to help with trust.

Healing Trust with Jasmine Essential Oil

Place a drop of oil of jasmine on the inside crease of your wrist in the middle. Place the inner wrist of the other hand on this spot so the two points are touching. Inhale the sweet fragrance.

Say the following:

"Thank you, Jasmine, for sharing your Divine Gifts. I receive into my being the Divine Gifts of Jasmine with love, gratitude, and appreciation.

"Thank you, Jasmine, for healing the broken trust in my ancestral lineage, healing the broken trust between me and the people in my life, and restoring trust in myself, in others, and in the Divine."

Breathe slowly while holding this point for a couple of minutes.

When you feel complete, thank Jasmine.

Repeat daily for several weeks.

 ## 7: WORKING WITH SELF-TRUST

When you delve deeper, you will discover there are times when you trusted yourself and all worked out. Here is an exercise to try.

For a few minutes, close your eyes and breathe deeply. Focus on your breath while doing the breathing pattern to slow down racing thoughts and relax your mind.

Now, remember a time in your life when you took a chance at trusting someone. You may have shared something near and dear to your heart with him or her. Maybe it was a business deal. Perhaps it was a choice you had to make to protect your child. Or a choice to let your child do something on her own without you taking charge.

How did that feel?

Now, remember a time when you found yourself faced with a challenging situation. What did you do to resolve the situation?

You got through it, didn't you? Now, pat yourself on the back. With your innate talents and heart wisdom, you have survived an ordeal by the choices you have made, and perhaps with the help of another person.

You are a lot more trusting than you think you are. Use this new-found awareness to rewrite your beliefs about trusting yourself, others, and the world.

SELF-REFLECTION PROMPTS

What does trust mean to you?

What situations or people are you most likely to trust? Why?

In what situations are you least likely to trust? Why?

How willing or unwilling are you to risk being vulnerable or hurt by another?

Do you trust yourself?

Are you willing to take a risk on yourself?

Do you believe you will make choices that support you?

How do you go about making choices? Do you rely upon your mind to "think" your way through a challenging situation?

Do you rely upon your gut instinct and go by what feels right?

Do you make choices by combining information with your intuition and gut feeling?

How do you discern who is a genuine friend?

Do you trust you can identify the best path to move forward?

What can you do today to strengthen your trust? Keep it simple and focus on the basics. Perhaps you could notice how you trust you will wake up in the morning. Or how you will have food and the resources you need to get through the day.

Notice how you unconsciously use trust during the day. This will strengthen your awareness of it. Also, notice how you thwart your ability to trust yourself through self-talk.

For example, when looking for a parking space, do you say, "I'll find one?" Or do you say, "I'll never find one?"

What happens when you turn your self-talk to trusting you will have what you seek?

In the following story about the Cat, the Crow, and Squirrel, we'll explore the many faces of fear.

THE MANY FACES OF FEAR

The Cat, the Crow, and the Squirrel

C at opened her eyes, angling her ears to catch the almost imperceptible scratch of nails on the tree bark. As she had done every day, she watched a young squirrel scamper up the tree trunk, run along a limb to the end, and begin to harvest cones. Cat's mottled tan-and-orange fur blended into the dappled shadows, where she lay very still on a large branch.

The squirrel didn't appear to notice her. With his back to Cat, he cut cones from the tree and let them drop to the ground below.

Foolish squirrel, Cat thought. *He'll make an excellent breakfast for me today.* She took a deep breath, considering whether stalking the tiny creature would be worth her while. She wasn't hungry. Not yet.

Squirrel slowly worked his way closer to her. Surprised he hadn't seen her, and ever so slowly, she gathered her legs under herself. *This is too easy*, she thought. *Let's have some fun.* She sneezed.

Squirrel froze mid-bite and scanned the tree. He didn't see Cat, whose immobile form blended into the tree trunk. As before, when Cat startled him, he scrambled to a higher branch.

Ah. The game begins, Cat thought. She had perfected the fine art of scaring her prey just enough to make them react but not so much that they bolted and ran out of reach.

By now, Squirrel had resumed his task but was more alert. Cat moved closer to the tree trunk.

"I've been watching you ever since you were born, Squirrel. You cannot escape me. I will catch you when you come down."

Frightened, Squirrel climbed higher into the tree where the branches were not so broad. The limb swayed when he ran to the end. He looked at Cat.

"Leave me alone. What have I done to harm you? Why must you torment me every day?"

Cat laughed. "I am a hunter. You are my prey. It's the way of life, Little One."

Squirrel reviewed his options. The neighboring tree was too far away. Could he drop to a limb below the cat and get away? What if he fell? It was a long way down, and a black cat stretched out amid the cones beneath the tree as if waiting for him to misstep and fall.

Just then, a crow landed nearby. The branch drooped ominously under the weight of the big bird, and Squirrel ran to the tree trunk.

Crow lowered his head toward Squirrel. "Don't be afraid of me," he croaked. He hopped closer to Squirrel. "I can help you escape that cat who wants to eat you." He hopped again. "Let me carry you to yonder tree, where you will be safe."

Squirrel looked to where the crow indicated. "That is the territory of Dog. He killed many of my family. I don't want to go there." Squirrel took several steps away from Crow.

"Then I can put you down on the ground and back with your family." Crow watched the youngster with his beady eyes. Suddenly, he leaped at the squirrel.

Squirrel raced higher up the tree trunk and clung to the bark.

Cat had climbed to the whirl of branches just below where the terrified creature perched. "I won't leave you to rot like Dog next door. I will eat every part of you, Squirrel, except your tail."

Angling for a share in the meal, Crow landed on the branch above Squirrel.

"Let me take you away from Cat, who would so mercilessly kill you. I will not harm you. I don't kill squirrels."

Squirrel looked from one predator to the other. His heart raced. He cried out to his parents. "Mother, Father, help me." Then he whined, "Leave me alone."

A flock of wrens landed in the tree near Squirrel. Madam Wren ruffled her feathers and called, "Leave him alone, Crow and Cat. You cannot have him until he has fulfilled his purpose. You know that. Why do you attempt to disrupt the natural order of things?" She landed in front of Crow. "You steal my eggs and my children."

"I have babies to raise too, Madam Wren. I do what I must."

"There is plenty of food, Crow. Just because you are bigger than us does not give you the right to attack us," she scolded. "Or this young one." With a flutter of wings, she landed near Cat. "Let him live. He is too scrawny to make a good meal for you. Let him grow and scatter the seeds of this tree so we will always have a home and plenty of food to thrive."

Cat's tail twitched. She knew Madam Wren was right but would never admit it. She swiped at Madam Wren with claws outstretched. The little bird flew out of range. The flock of wrens started chirping, raising such a ruckus that it hurt Cat's ears. Crow flew off, muttering, "I'll be back for you, Squirrel, and steal every last seed you collect."

Flattening her ears, Cat backed down the trunk. "I will let you live today, Squirrel, but tomorrow, be wary. I will be watching you like an invisible shadow. You will never know when I will strike or where. I know all your hiding places. You will never be free of your fear of me." She returned to her favorite perch in the tree. The corners of Cat's lips curved up. "I am queen here."

Squirrel returned to his task. His was a life of peril, never knowing when death would strike or who its deliverer would be. Yet, he had a task to perform, and, ever watchful, he went about completing it.

Crow, however, was not content to watch and approached Squirrel once more. "Let us make a bargain. I will keep you safe from Cat, Dog, and Eagle. In exchange, you will work for me, giving me the seeds you collect. You may keep just enough to sustain your life so you can work for me. I get the rest." Crow edged closer to Squirrel. "Don't you see? We both win."

Squirrel shook his head. "Crow, I must also provide for my family and stock up for winter. If I give you everything I gather, we will all perish. You win. We lose. No, I will not make a bargain with you."

"Then you will die, Squirrel."

"You cannot steal from others in an attempt to prolong the inevitable. Shedding this earthly form is the way of life, Crow. You know that. Now go. I have work to do."

Squirrel bared his teeth at Crow and lunged.

Crow flew away with a startled *caw*.

Squirrel grew older, mated, and had many children and grandchildren. He taught his children to face danger and not let fear stop them from playing their part in the natural order. Crow and Cat continued to harass his family. He defended them valiantly but was not always successful. One day, when Squirrel was old and slow, one of Crow's children swooped and caught him as he raced along a bare branch. It was his time.

THE HEALER'S PATH: ELLARA'S WISDOM

The Many Faces of Fear

The biggest threat to our freedom and sovereignty is fear. Fear infects our lives, minds, and hearts like a deadly, invisible disease. Fear creates self-doubt and mistrust and disconnects us from the Divine within. This primal emotion provides an opportunity for each of us to recognize our true nature.

Like Crow and Cat, the perpetrators of fear are crafty. The dark forces in our world thrive on our fearful responses to the threatening situations we encounter. They know just what to say or do to trigger uncertainty about the future. The unseen culprits make laws that destroy our freedoms and incite emotions that cloud our judgment and ability to think clearly, just like Cat and Crow.

Do you remember the stories we heard when the Natuan mercenary commander swept into our country ten years ago? Nana Magog mimicked his tinny voice where he declared he was here to save us from a terrible threat coming from another part of the world. Nana Magog saw through his deceit. She laughed and said, "The Commander speaks with two tongues. He speaks charismatic words that please his listeners. He uses a smokescreen to deflect resistance as he chases after illusions of wealth and power. He is not here to 'save' us but to conquer us. *He* is the terrible threat."

Fear affects everyone, including those trained in understanding psychic warfare—and yes, even me. Daily, the words and actions of others bombard us. There is great power in words. They possess the power to uplift. They can drag us down, or become a curse like those words Doyen Camila pronounced when I went to the Gra'Bandia Council meeting at Cuilithe.

Words can stimulate feelings of love. They can activate our primal survival reflexes. People say many things. Some of their words make sense. Others don't. Some people advocate with persuasive words for a specific law, proclaim their support for women's equality, or of protecting the environment.

The dark force agents reveal their true intentions through their actions. Glib of tongue, they wax eloquent about the benefits of a new law or product. Yet, as they weave persuasion into their empty promises, they steal citizens' freedoms and rights, ruin economies, fabricate shortages, and much more.

The Natuan commander in Araval proclaims he is defending the Alban citizens against invaders. Yet since his arrival, Commander Grath has forced new ordinances upon us that quietly erode women's freedoms and rights. These documents with vaguely worded laws allow his officers to interpret the decrees as it suits them.

Captain Sengy came to Sheldon to uphold laws that declared women could not own businesses. No decree was made, but that didn't stop Captain Sengy and his men from pillaging Sara's goldsmith shop.

We, the citizens of Alba, suffer. We don't like it, but as a peaceful people, we are reluctant to rebel. Nobody planned the rebellion that occurred in Sheldon and resulted in Sam's and Captain Sengy's death.

Of course, the fearmongers have a solution that satisfies their hidden agenda. These solutions often mean going against our inner knowing and forfeiting our integrity and freedom.

If you relate to the world through your mind or can see patterns, you can analyze a set of statements, actions, and behaviors. With discernment, you can notice if there are flaws in logic or inconsistencies between what the leaders say and what they do.

When in doubt, observe a person's actions. Taking physical action on a commitment or promise takes more effort than talking. The truth lies in what a person does more than the wants, wishes, and illusions of which they speak. Even though the ability to discern incongruous patterns is a useful tool, it is still an interpretation by the mind and can often be overridden by what we *think* we want. We can also ignore the whispered wisdom from our bodies and heart. Listening to our hearts will provide a more reliable guide than listening to our minds or the persuasive words of others.

Some of us are designed to have a gut response to our outer world. Related to instinct, a gut response is an instant knowing. Instinct is what you use in a survival situation when you sense something is wrong in your environment and must take immediate action. Instinct tells you to run from the bear.

For personal choices, like what to eat, or what clothes to wear, a gut response shines. An external stimulus usually triggers both reactions, which are a form of inner guidance.

Pay attention when you start to feel confused, disbelieving, and uneasy. A part of you is sensing disharmony. Your instincts, gut responses, and intuition will help you determine the best action to take. You will need a clear mind and an open heart. Meditation is called a practice for a reason. Clearing your mind allows you to listen to your instincts and discern whether a person or organization is being truthful or if they have something to hide. Develop trust in your ability to discern the connection between persuasive words and unsavory actions.

APPLYING ELLARA'S WISDOM

Discerning the Truth Daily Practices

8: Understand Your Body's Messages

Your body is wise and can become your best teacher and distiller of the truth. But to do this, you have to understand what you feel in your body at any given time. This takes time and practice, so be patient with yourself. The goal is to notice how different situations affect your body's responses. Experiment with the following exercise and jot down what you notice.

Sit or lie in a quiet place. Nature is best.

Take slow, deep breaths. Inhale to the count of four heartbeats. Exhale slowly to the count of six or eight heartbeats. Do this several times. As you exhale, invite your mind to release its thoughts.

Imagine you have strong roots that extend deep into the earth. Send them to the core of the planet and wrap them around a golden ring anchored into the crystal core. Alternatively, imagine you have roots like a tree. Send your roots deep into the earth and wrap them around rocks to anchor and ground yourself firmly. Energize this connection with your breath. Notice how your awareness shifts from your mind into your body.

Now, notice your heart. Does it feel open and expansive or closed and guarded?

Remember something that makes you feel joyful, like a beautiful sunset or a baby animal. What do you feel in your heart and body? Does the energy around your heart expand? Does your life force flow smoothly through your body?

Now, think of something that upsets you. How do your heart and body respond? Do you notice tension, rigidity in your form, and a stifling of your energy flow? Do you stop breathing?

Practice this several times to get a strong sense of your body's responses to uplifting or stressful thoughts and events.

Now, in your mind's eye, play out a short segment of a situation that has already happened. Or a situation you expect in the future. How do your heart and body respond?

End your practice sessions with thoughts that uplift you and open your heart.

Your body gives you reliable, instantaneous responses to every situation. The hard part is to keep your mind from jumping to conclusions or analyzing what you experienced. The mind can distort what you feel or dismiss it as silly, fanciful, and untrue.

When this happens, thank your mind. Return to your body and the present moment by breathing deeply, focusing your attention, and noticing every detail of something around you. This could be something you see, hear, or feel.

SELF-REFLECTION PROMPTS

Take this practice out into the world. Listen to the people around you. Watch as events unfold. How does your body respond?

Have you noticed inconsistencies between what someone says and what they do? It could be something like promising to give up certain foods, drinking, or smoking, but they never do. Or they may say they are respectful or tolerant but act superior or judgmental toward someone. Or any number of things.

How do you sense it?

Where have you been inconsistent with your words and actions? It could be with small things like eating something you promised yourself you would not or saying yes to something when you really want to say no.

What is your definition of truth?

Are there Universal truths? Subjective truths?

Can you tell the difference?

Universal truths apply to everyone and to all life. Subjective truths are your personal truths, created by your personal beliefs, and social and religious conditioning. They may or may not align with Universal truths.

What are signals from your body that let you know something aligns with the truth? Where in your body do you feel it?

What are signs from your body that something *misaligns* with the truth? Where do you feel it?

Do you notice your gut response?

Can you tell when someone is trying to deceive you? A little? A lot? What do you notice that lets you know?

How can you tell when someone is being authentic?

How does your body feel when someone shares beliefs that run counter to what you perceive as the truth?

When you encounter a person who does not share your beliefs, can you step back and find common ground with that person? Remember, we are all part of the Divine.

What can you do today to strengthen your ability to discern the truth? You can train yourself to notice physical cues from your body, like a constricted throat or a relaxed state. Investigate what doesn't sound right to you. Pay more attention to what is said and what is done, and notice how well they align.

Believing in yourself goes a long way toward finding your place in the world, as illustrated in the following story.

WEALTH AND ABUNDANCE: A REFLECTION OF SELF-WORTH

The Grimalkin Cub and the Jackal

L ast to be birthed, the grimalkin cub struggled to crawl to her mother's breast. When she arrived, her two siblings wouldn't let her suckle.

"You're too small and weak," her older sister said.

"Mother can only feed the two of us. If we let you eat, you will take our food, and we won't become powerful hunters. We will die." Her brother rolled so that he blocked access to their mother's teats.

The youngest cub couldn't muscle her way to the food, so she waited until her siblings had fallen asleep. Her mother shifted so she could get some milk, but her older littermates had drained the supply, and she only ate half a meal.

Her mother's raspy tongue stroked her body. "Don't worry, Little One. If the Goddess wills it, you will survive and thrive."

Days passed into weeks, and her brother and sister grew into strong, healthy cubs. Not so Runt, as the youngsters called her. But she got enough to eat and also grew. Yet, she never felt welcomed by her siblings. They made fun of her and pointed out how much smaller and weaker she was compared to them.

"You're all black. You don't even look like us," they said. "We look like Mother. You'll never accomplish what we can."

She didn't play with her littermates. When she tried, they tumbled her over and over to prove she was inferior. They pushed her aside when Mother Grimalkin brought fresh meat. Despite her smaller size, she growled at her brother and swatted at him, smacking him in the nose. She didn't give up easily, despite her brother's taunts.

"It's a hard world," her brother said, pushing her aside. "You had just as well find out now. You'll be prey for some hunter."

"Let her eat," Grimalkin Mother would remind her offspring. "She may not look like you, but we are a family. One day, you will be grateful for that." She growled at her son. "Move over."

Runt's brother moved his tawny, brown-rosetted body slightly so Runt could edge in and eat from the less nutritious part of the beast. Her brother growled softly to Runt, "You live only because of Mother's generosity."

Runt's will to live was strong. She was a clever young grimalkin, learning to rely upon other traits of her species than speed and brawn. Observing her siblings and the animals around their den for extended periods helped her develop patience. She often stole behind her mother to watch her hunt. Runt watched for each creature's strengths and weaknesses, and soon she could predict an animal's behavior.

One day, her mother went hunting, and the three young cubs were told to stay close to their home. But Runt's brother, the more adventurous of the trio, strayed far from their den. Runt's sister went with him. Runt followed, but she was not as fast and lagged behind. The young cubs went to the water hole.

Runt stayed concealed in a hollow log hidden by a scrubby bush. She had often come to the water hole to quietly observe the activities of the other animals while her mother was away. She knew every creature that came to drink. This was the time of day when the jackal family owned the pool.

In their ignorance, her siblings strutted to the water and hunched to lap up the cool water.

It was not long before Jackal, leader of the pack, noticed the intruders. The jackals stalked around the youngsters.

"Who do you think you are, drinking our water?" their leader barked. The pack pressed around the two inexperienced cubs, who huddled together.

Runt's sister lifted her head and scanned the area. "Mother," she called. "Mother!"

"Your mother won't come for you," Jackal huffed. He sniffed along the neck of one cub. "We killed her. And you will make a delicious snack for our children."

The small pack drew closer, snarling and snapping at the youngsters.

Runt, who had spent hours watching the animals at the pool, knew what Jackal said was untrue. If they had killed their mother, they would have eaten her and would be full, not stalking her brother and sister.

The cubs glanced at each other, brows furrowed.

"Kill them," Jackal said.

Runt wanted to help, but words reminding her she would become easy prey played through her mind. While she wrestled with what to do, the jackals attacked her siblings. The cubs cried in pain, slashing at their attackers with outstretched claws. Even though the jackals were not much bigger than the two grimalkin cubs, there were more of them. They harried the youngsters mercilessly, snapping at their hind legs and leaping for their throats.

Finally, Runt couldn't endure their wails any longer and roared as she had heard her mother roar. The jackals paused in the fight and looked around nervously. Runt crawled from her hiding place and positioned herself so the sun was behind her, casting a long shadow that made her look big. She stalked toward the jackal pack and roared again. Without the help of the hollow log, though, it sounded small.

The jackals laughed. They swarmed around her. "You're half the size of the others. You'll be much easier to kill."

Runt's siblings climbed shakily to their feet, shook themselves, and bounded away. Alone, she faced the jackals, knowing they would kill her if she ran.

They circled her warily, saying, "You don't even look like a predator. You'll never amount to anything. You deserve to die so we may live and thrive."

The young grimalkin watched. Their words reminded her of those uttered by her brother and sister. Yet here she was, alive. She had saved her siblings so they could live another day. She could sacrifice herself and let the jackals kill her so they could feed their family. But Runt noticed the jackals didn't move against her.

She lifted her head, flattening her ears, and fixed her gaze on the leader like she had seen her mother do.

"If I am so unworthy of living, then kill me now." Boldly, she took a step toward Jackal. "Why don't you make good your threat?"

Jackal backed away, his attention divided between Runt and the shrubs behind her. He sniffed the air warily.

Runt twitched her tail. Behind her, two jackals crept closer, unaware of the fierce threat lurking in the bushes. In a flash, Runt whirled and slashed them across the nose. They yelped and retreated.

"Call off your pack, Jackal." She took another step toward the leader.

He backed away until his hind feet splashed into the water.

Then, a full-throated roar came from behind Runt, along with the thud of running feet on the packed earth. The jackals fled.

Runt's mother stood protectively over her and scolded, "Daughter, you and your siblings have disobeyed my instructions. This put all of you in danger. You should not have challenged Jackal."

"But I was defending my brother and sister," Runt protested. "And you came."

Her mother touched Runt with her nose, then licked the dusky-colored fur along the cub's head and back. "I commend your courage, but you are no match for the jackals. You are lucky to survive. You can't count on me always being there for you." Her gaze swept the watering hole. "You did well. Never let anyone tell you that you are weak or unworthy because you are different. What you lack in strength and agility, you make up for in courage and intelligence. One day, you will have a family. You will rival me in your hunting talent." A branch snapped in the tangle of shrubs on the far side of the pool.

Grimalkin Mother lifted her head and sniffed. The tip of her tail twitched. "Go home, now," she said to Runt.

Her mother walked partly around the pool before she looked back at the youngster. She sighed. "Come. Help me hunt the oryx. We will feast on one tonight."

The Healer's Path: Ellara's Wisdom

Self-worth and Abundance

Despite what others may say, like the grimalkin cub, we have more abilities than we give ourselves credit for. When we do not feel worthy and deserving, it is hard to see and accept our gifts. Our vision narrows, and it is hard to find the many blessings and abundance around us. Wealth and abundance come from within, from our perceptions about ourselves and our worth. Your outer world success relates to how much you believe in yourself and accept and appreciate your native talents and abilities.

Those raised in the Goddess tradition already understand the infinite abundance surrounding us. Plentiful resources allow us to rise above our survival needs and pursue more significant levels of consciousness and spiritual growth. However, some of us may not be as familiar with this awareness, and some of us may have forgotten it.

Wealth is a mindset tied to our sense of worthiness. Our concepts of wealth and abundance are woven into the fabric of our being and affect our perception of ourselves. When we do not value ourselves, we look outside for what we are missing within. Perceived lack can make us feel unworthy, unsuccessful, undeserving, and unlovable. Then we strive to get whatever we can, becoming consumed by greed. We seek to fill the void with material possessions. But it is empty wealth, an illusion.

Success, wealth, and abundance might not look like material possessions, power, and control.

What if wealth and abundance come from the heart instead?

What if true wealth means having the time and freedom to do what makes your heart sing, to be with those you love, to be healthy, and to feel fulfilled?

Imagine that you are quietly sitting in a meadow, observing the nature around you. Or venture into your garden, park, or forest.

Notice how the wild animals eat. For them, food is abundant, and their natural instincts keep it that way. Do you see how the deer browse on a few blackberry leaves, then move to another set of bushes? And the rabbit eats a few stalks of greens, then hops on? Observe the flock of blackbirds as they swoop to the ground *en masse*, forage for bugs in the grass, then depart just as abruptly.

Part of their behavior stems from being prey animals. They don't remain long in one place where they can be vulnerable to predators. More importantly, they don't eat so many leaves or bugs that they deplete the population or kill the plants. The animals prune and fertilize the vegetation, stimulating fresh growth. It is a symbiotic relationship. One of mutual, unspoken agreements that benefits all.

Notice how many blades of grass there are and the abundant number of herbs, weeds, shrubs, brush, and trees. Plants take nutrients from the earth and, together with sunlight, they grow. The flora creates oxygen in the air we breathe, which animals, including us, need to live. This is one example of the beautiful complexity of the Goddess's Order at work for the benefit of all.

We are the stewards of the land and our world. Awareness of how we use natural resources comes from understanding that every part of nature has a role.

Have you noticed that when populations disrespect the natural cycles, there are shortages and dead zones where life no longer thrives? In the Divine Order of our world, the Goddess works to keep the balance. She sends birds and members of the rodent family to carry seeds from thriving regions. In time, the deprived environment flourishes again.

Have you noticed this where you live? Even in densely populated cities, wildlife still exists. Have you seen intrepid dandelions, blackberries, and horsetail—some of the hardiest members of the plant kingdom—push their way between cracks in the stones?

Our planet is abundant. It thrives. It is up to us, with our daily practices and desires, to live so that we do not deplete our natural resources and allow room for nature to grow. Take a little. Give a little. That is the nature of abundance.

What if we appreciated all the surrounding abundance? What if we respected the land and each other? Would we need to fight over who controls resources? When we curb our material appetites and desires—our thoughts and beliefs—and shift our perception of wealth, can we acknowledge all the abundance around us?

Do you see the natural wealth around you? Even in urban areas, do you hear the songbirds and see the crows and robins? Do you hear the shrill call of eagles and hawks? Hear the wind in the trees? See the beauty in flowers?

Self-worth and Wealth

Our perception of wealth—or lack thereof—starts with how we feel about ourselves. Without a strong sense of our self-worth, we often compare ourselves to others. We measure our accomplishments and accumulations against what another has. This leads to a perpetuation of unworthiness and pressure to succeed, no matter the cost. This path does not serve us and often leads to wars over resources and feuds over who is more successful, influential, or prestigious than someone else. It leads to expressions of power and control over others and circumstances. It opens us up to people who would deceive us. Those practices may work for the short term but are not sustainable without escalating to higher levels of manipulation, intimidation, and fear to maintain control. This is the pattern of those who are greedy and speak lies to manipulate others like the merchant tried with Sara.

One day, Margot and I were at Sara's goldsmith shop when a newly arrived merchant from Langon swaggered in. He dressed in a tailored wool coat over a silk frilled shirt. Beneath long fine wool trousers, he wore soft leather boots. A bright sash girded his ample waist, and rubies, emeralds, and diamonds flashed in the sunlight from every finger.

He scanned the displays of necklaces, pendants, bracelets, and pins artfully crafted from gold, silver, and gemstones.

He nodded as he caressed an exquisite wide band. "Nice work," he said in a deep voice that vibrated the air. "Perhaps we can make a bargain."

Sara watched the man warily. Her teenage daughter, Katarine, and Margot stopped sorting bits of gold and stones into trays at the back of the shop. They looked ready to pounce on the man if he made a false move.

"What do you have in mind?" Sara asked.

With a dramatic display, the man pulled a large, folded pouch from inside his coat and lay it on the counter. Before he opened it, he tapped the fabric and said, "What I have here is priceless. I would be willing to trade you one of these for this bracelet and a few other of your pieces."

We waited for him to reveal his priceless goods.

But he continued, "I've traveled the world over to find these. They are from the elusive Weyverin tribes south of Zimbrel. No one has ever traded with these reclusive inhabitants before. And probably will never again. These magical artifacts are incredibly rare. Imagine how priceless your jewelry would be if you used these. You could become the wealthiest craftswoman in the region. In your country."

Sara shifted to her other foot and leaned on the counter. "Don't keep us in suspense. Show us what you have."

Smiling, the man placed his hand over the pouch. He scanned the room again. With calculated deliberation, he unfolded one layer, but the goods remained concealed.

After a moment, Sara turned away. "I have a commission to finish. I'm not interested."

The man seemed to expect this. He turned to me. "These magical items will make your life flow smoothly." He leaned forward and whispered loudly, "They can make the Natuan clerics leave." He pressed on. "Think about how easily you will do your work without the clerics hunting you. Don't you think your life will be much happier and freer?" He tapped the pouch. "These are your ticket to freedom from persecution. For all of you."

Sara interrupted him. "The Goddess will take care of the clerics." She moved to the table where she worked. "I'm not interested. Take your precious wares elsewhere."

The man straightened. "You are rejecting the very thing that can save your island from the impending threat you face. I'm only trying to help you save your people."

Sara returned to the counter. "I forgive you because you do not appear to know our ways." She started to shove the partly opened pouch away but snatched her hand back as if bitten by a viper. She stared at the pouch. "Take that unholy relic from my shop this instant." She snatched up her small forge poker.

The man opened his mouth to say more.

"Now."

The man scooped up his bundle and tucked it away. Sara followed him to the door. "Get back on that ship from which you came and leave Sheldon. You are not welcome here."

One has to be firm with a person who would deceive you. This merchant picked the wrong person to swindle. He left on the next tide.

Sara's artwork brings beauty into the world. People are naturally drawn to beautiful things, bringing a measure of heartfelt fulfillment.

For others who strive to become rich in money and possessions, wealth can be a mask that hides feelings of unworthiness. These individuals may present themselves as successful, the master of their craft, and knowledgeable to the point of arrogance. In positions of influence, they tend to be self-centered, narcissistic, and care only for what they can gain. Carefully concealing this attitude with charm and persuasive helpfulness, they claim they are your powerful ally. They can easily shift toward bullying and intimidation when things don't go their way. This mask hides the shadow side of self-worth. Does this sound like the crafty perpetrators of fear that I talked about earlier? I want to suggest that the Droc'ri are lacking in self-worth, and that affects how they go through life.

Even though we know about their power-hungry tactics, their influence on us is often unconscious, leading us to question our worth. After all, if another person has a big house, lots of gold, horses, servants, and wears beautiful clothes while we are living more humbly, we unconsciously question why we can't have those luxuries, too.

Each person has his or her own definition of wealth. This definition is directly tied to what that person perceives as his or her individual value. For example, a person who identifies with education, intimate discussions, and philosophical debates about the Goddess or the meaning of life may measure her value by how educated she is and how well she can debate these topics.

Another person, who is more materially oriented, may value creature comforts and measure his or her worth by what she has accumulated.

Another person's perception of wealth and prosperity could be connected to their physical strength and robust health. Or of having the time and freedom to follow what makes their heart sing. And for others, it could be traveling, connection to the Goddess, or loving relationships.

One more aspect influences how we value ourselves; what other people say to and about us.

When we operate from a position of lowered self-worth, we look out-side ourselves for validation and valuation. We let others determine what they will pay us, even if we secretly disagree. We measure our success by the successes of others. Fear of ridicule holds us back from sharing our ideas. We contort ourselves to fit in. We please others so we can be seen as indispensable, and we secretly hope to make the other person value us more. Safety and survival factor into this as well.

The problem with this belief system is that, like the small grimalkin, we sacrifice ourselves unnecessarily for the sake of obtaining valida-tion from others. When we acknowledge our strengths and our gifts, then we will find a place of belonging in the community, even with our differences.

Judging and ridiculing differences is another way that those who hide their lagging self-worth try to look superior. The unspoken implication is: if you are not like me, then you don't belong and, therefore, you have no value.

Of course, this premise is false. It is our differences, our unique combination of traits, talents, and abilities, that give us value and make each of us an indispensable part of a community and of the world.

Our value is not limited to just what we have accumulated, whether mentally or physically. It is something beyond this realm. Remember earlier when we talked about being a fragment of the Goddess in a human form? How can you put a price on that?

What if you are enough just as you are? What if you are exactly as you are supposed to be?

Your true value comes from remembering your Divine nature and the gifts you have to share with others. Everything else is what makes life interesting and fun.

APPLYING ELLARA'S WISDOM

Self-Worth and Abundance Daily Practices

9: Noticing Abundance

Find a comfortable place in nature. It could be a woodland, a park, or even your garden. It can be any place where you step away from the busy world to the quiet of nature around you. A rooftop in the city. Or even looking out your window.

Calm your mind with your breath.

Soften your gaze and take in your environment.

What colors do you see? How many shades and variations of each color are there?

What do you hear? Can you identify the sounds?

What do you feel?

Notice the vegetation, the trees, the grasses, herbs, leaves, and flowers. Can you count them?

Notice all the various life forms around you—animals, birds, insects, reptiles, rocks, and so forth.

Notice the wildflowers, the pebbles, and the grains of sand.

Take some deep breaths. Notice how available air is.

Enjoy noticing the abundance all around you.

How does that make you feel?

Our world has everything we need to thrive.

10: Self-Worth Practice

Let's go on a brief journey to explore your self-worth.

Find a comfortable place to sit or lie down, free from interruptions.

Take some breaths to calm your mind and relax your body.

Feel yourself settling into the chair, floor, or ground, merging your energy with it, and being fully supported.

In your mind's eye, imagine you are a spark of energy. Imagine this is your bit of soul.

Take a closer look. What do you see?

What do you feel?

Do you have a sense that you are beyond time and form?

Ask your soul if she has a message for you.

11: Self-worth Daily Practice

As a daily practice, list five things you accomplished today. Then, note what gift you used. It could be several.

Next, say, "I am grateful for all my gifts and abilities, and they are grateful for me.

"I am grateful for all I have, and all I have is grateful for me.

"I am grateful I am enough, just as I am, and being enough is grateful for me.

"I am grateful I am an expression of the Divine, and the Divine is grateful for me."

The goal is for you to see you are more than your physical accomplishments. Your value is in who you are. You share your gifts with the world automatically, just by living.

SELF-REFLECTION PROMPTS

What is your definition of wealth and abundance?

What does that look like?

What brings meaning to your life? Be specific.

What can you do to bring more meaning to your life now?

How do you feel about yourself?

Do you judge yourself? If so, what do you tell yourself?

How are you different from others?

How have your differences affected your life?

What would it take for you to fully embrace what makes you unique?

What gifts do you have to share with the world?

To what degree are you doing so?

What is holding you back?

Do you feel worthy and valuable?

What areas of your life are affected by feeling less than or deserving?

How does your sense of self-worth relate to the abundance you perceive in your life?

What shift in your attitudes and perceptions can you make to witness the abundance in which you are immersed?

How can you shift your definition of wealth and abundance?

What would be a new definition?

What can you do to start living this new definition?

How can you prosper with what you have now?

What shifts in beliefs would be required?

What is one step you can take today to strengthen your self-value? Perhaps it could be witnessing what the little voice in your head is saying, then asking whose voice is speaking. Is it your parent, a teacher, or someone influential in your life? Perhaps it could be doing something supportive for yourself, such as taking some time alone or going for a walk.

What if you could use your special gifts and magical talents like Mirala and Galen in the next story?

THE BLESSING OF EMPATHS

Mirala and Galen

Heavy, dark clouds swept steadily closer, moving more swiftly than usual. Tension laced the air as women and men labored to harvest and store the grain and straw before rain rotted their crops. Already, the first large raindrops were falling.

A slender woman stood at the edge of the field. Long black hair billowed around her calm, ageless face in the rising wind. Deliberately, Mirala raised her arms skyward, as if embracing the approaching storm and sang a simple melody—over and over—until she matched the tone of the tempest. Time stood still. So did the approaching weather, and her people raced to complete their tasks.

A man stood behind the Seeress, his gaze shifting between the woman, the dark clouds, and his village mates. Galen shifted from foot to foot and tugged on his belt. He knew better than to interfere.

Before his eyes, the clouds lifted and brightened. The oppressive air thinned and dissolved. He waited.

The song stopped. Galen rushed to support Mirala as she crumbled to the ground. She panted, pale-faced, and her body trembled. Gently, Galen cradled her. Calling upon the earth elementals for assistance, he drew from her the energies Mirala had absorbed from the storm to dissolve them into the earth.

Finally, she opened her eyes and gazed into his.

"This storm was more powerful than the last," Galen admonished. "You will kill yourself one day if you keep taking the spirit of the tempest into yourself. What if I am not here to restore you?"

Mirala touched his cheek. "You worry too much, Galen." She sat up. "You use earth magic. Can you teach me how to transmute a force such as this storm into something beneficial?"

Galen shook his head. "What you ask is beyond what I know."

"Then let's discover it together."

Over the next few moon cycles, Galen and Mirala explored their respective strengths. Each expanded the other's talents.

Practicing Mirala's ability to sense subtle energies and glean insights, Galen learned more from the earth elementals with which he was strongly connected. His magic became stronger, and his healing talent more effective.

Mirala witnessed how Galen commanded the respect of the elementals and how they willingly served him and helped him accomplish what he wanted.

One day, she asked, "What if I combine my ability to feel deeply, to take in the essence of the threat, and instead of trying to transmute it within my body, as I have done in the past, I ask for your elementals help in transforming it?"

It wasn't long before their community encountered another threat. Snow blanketed the land. The village food stores ran low, and the animals they usually hunted had moved on. The villagers pleaded with Mirala to do something.

Mirala and Galen left their home and climbed a nearby mountain. Clustered at one end of the white valley were the black circular huts of their village from which rose thin gray wisps of smoke.

"I've stopped storms and floods. I don't know if I can make the snow melt and the animals return." Mirala shivered.

Galen put an arm around her. "I understand. I can heal a broken limb or bless the land so our crops grow, but I don't know, either. Let's get warm. Maybe the fire elementals will inspire us."

They built a small fire and heated water. Mirala placed herbs to steep in a stone bowl. They drank the brew and watched the dancing flames.

"I have an idea." Mirala stood and surveyed the valley.

Above her, broken clouds offered bits of blue sky and an occasional glimpse of the sun. She raised her hands to the sky. She started singing an uplifting melody, rising through musical notes until she found one that resonated with the rays of sunshine. Drawing upon how Galen summoned the elementals, she commanded the fire, drawing symbols with her hands. She invited the Fire of the Sun to fill her. Then she expanded it outward. The snow where she stood melted. Immediately, she strode down the mountain, snow melting wherever she stepped.

Galen trotted behind her. When they reached the valley floor, arm in arm, they walked back and forth on all the trails and through the meadows. Mirala melted the snow. Grasses, herbs, and weeds sprang up behind Galen. As if called by the wind, the wild animals returned to feed on the verdant growth.

The villagers flocked around them, singing words of praise and offering them bowls of stew. Soon, other villagers came to their valley to forage for food, and word spread about Mirala and Galen. Many villages sought their help. Galen and Mirala willingly shared their talents. They returned to the mountaintop often and rekindled the fire in honor of its essence that had inspired and transformed Mirala's abilities.

The Healer's Path: Ellara's Wisdom

The Blessing of Empaths

Healing empaths, like Galen and Mirala, are more common than you may think. Each of us has this capability. Like Mirala and Galen, we have specialties, areas where we take in and transmute energies.

As a child, were you aware of the energies around you? Could you sense your home's atmosphere and your parents' mood? Did you avoid certain places or people? Did you know why you avoided them? Were you aware of ghosts in your house? Was your wisdom valued and your intuitive hunches respected by those around you?

Or did you grow up like me?

I was keenly aware of the subtle energies around me, but no one explained how these invisible forces worked. I felt safe around the animals. When Nana Magog and my mother had angry words in another room, I often ran to my secret hideout in the woods. Shapes in the dark scared me. I picked up pain and emotions from other people and felt them in my body, but I didn't know what they were. Certain there was something wrong with me, I was often sickly, and Nana had to heal me many times.

It wasn't until I was much older that I sorted out my natural state from what I felt from others. It took even longer to identify *what* I felt and to trust it was not just the product of a prolific, fanciful imagination.

When I was seven years old, a crate fell on Sam, severely injuring him. It was many months before I saw him again. When he came to our house, I was delighted to see him. But when I hugged him, I cried out in pain. For an instant, I couldn't move, and when I did, the pain was excruciating. I thought he was hurting me and pushed away from him, but the pain didn't go away. Confused, I clung to him, and he to me. I hurt for the duration of his visit. A day or two after he left, the pain subsided, but my sense of it lingered. Nana Magog or my mother never explained it. Eventually, I put two and two together and realized the discomfort I felt was from another person. I started paying more attention to how I felt around people after that.

This is what it means to be an empath—feeling, seeing, hearing, smelling, and knowing with your second sight. Some of us take in the pain and suffering of others to transmute. It is our way to heal—to make whole—another person, community, or the world. We make the best Healers, craftspeople, and advocates.

Some people are not as sensitive to energies, sounds, and the senses. Just like developing talent as a Healer, we can cultivate sensitivity with dedication and consistent practice. For other people, the gift comes already developed. Some in this group view their hyper senses as a curse and try to shut the ability off. That rarely works. When our nervous system is designed to connect more deeply to our surroundings, we can try to block the input, but it does not go away. Often, the best path forward is to harness this gift and use it to aid others.

Scholars postulate that highly sensitive people comprise about one-fifth of our population. Like canaries in a mine, we play an essential role in the survival of our world, sensing what others either don't see or choose to ignore. We identify imbalances in the environment or among our communities long before others. We access more information than most and process that information more thoroughly. Our minds are perpetually busy. We tend to be loners, and it's imperative that the people we spend time with have supportive and harmonic energies. We need time alone, especially in nature, to reclaim our sense of self.

Our highly sensitive nature fits around each of us like a friendly blanket, influencing and enhancing the talents we were born with. Our empathic ability interfaces with the environment and people, helping us to forge strong bonds and a deep understanding of those we encounter.

But if you grew up like me in a household that frowned on any extraordinary abilities, you don't understand the value of your ability. You discard it as unimportant, and your intuitive and empathic gifts become an annoyance. Your gifts go underground, yet you live with subtle nudges that help to keep you safe. People say you are lucky. You think your luck has nothing to do with your intuitive capabilities and deny your empathic nature. However, rationalize as you might, you can't explain how you know things.

When we understand and interpret what we receive, we become effective Healers. Sensing and interpreting energies can help us foretell events, excel at our chosen professions, and guide those less aware into the future. Empaths see beyond the physical into the realms where we are all connected. Sometimes, we forget our significance and hide our talents to conform to societal norms.

Empaths can become overwhelmed with the many bits of information we continually receive and process. Sometimes we shut it off and ignore what we sense. That is like putting a sack over our heads. The sensations still come in. We still feel them, and they can unconsciously affect our well-being, health, and state of mind. Other times, we pick up things but don't know what they mean.

No matter how you see your empathic abilities, know that they are divinely given. They are an important part of your life.

Applying Ellara's Wisdom

Exploring Your Empathic Nature Daily Practices

Here is a way to discern what you sense and help you trust your intuition. An important prerequisite is to calm the mind. Reducing the parade of thoughts and inner chatter through a breathing practice can become the doorway that connects you to your senses. Drumming or chanting can also calm the mind.

Shifting into a more relaxed state of being is an important first step before moving on to sense another person's energies or the energies of the environment. It becomes easier the more you understand your native state of being, which is most easily attained by noticing how you relate to the world when you are alone. Empaths are naturally oriented to receiving.

Even if you tend to be outward-moving and other-oriented—doing things for others—and are perpetually busy, you still have the ability to receive. You can refine this ability by taking the time to *consciously* receive. Receiving can take many forms, as you will see.

12: Clearing Other's Energies

When we are with people, our energy fields touch and merge. That is how we can sense when someone is not feeling well, is angry, or is happy. We grow up around people, and their energy can become imprinted into our aura so that certain energies feel normal and comfortable. Unconsciously, we identify with their energetic and emotional patterns, and this can become an emotional baseline.

Close and comfortable as they might feel, another person's energetic patterns are not yours. You have distinct energetic patterns and can learn to identify patterns that are not yours. You already do so unconsciously. Do you find yourself tense around someone? Does your back hurt, or does your throat feel scratchy? Most of us go through life not realizing that everything we feel or think is mostly from outside us and is not ours. The more conscious you can become of the energetic patterns you sense, the easier it is to separate them from your aura.

This topic is more easily talked about than recognized in daily life. Have you ever been to a gathering where the group's enthusiasm for an idea or action is high? You join in and are ready to march. Yet after you leave and the group energy dissipates, you wonder what possessed you to become so enthusiastic about something you don't like at all!

As I said before, we are entangled in other people's energy fields, which means we have access to others' thoughts, feelings, fears, wants, and desires. It is easy to believe these are our thoughts and desires and act upon them, even if they are not in our best interest.

Clearing Your Energy Field

Once you recognize your natural emotional and energetic states, you can clear other people's energies from yourself. When you do, you will immediately feel better and return to your natural stable state.

You will want to clear your energy field before consciously working with a person, animal, or place, so your own energies don't distort what you receive or the energies you transmit for healing. Clear it again after you have completed the work.

I use a simple prayer request to clear unwanted energy. Feel free to adapt the wording.

"Divine Beloved, please clear from me all thought forms, emotional, physical, and spiritual patterns I have received from others. Clear any energies that are not mine. Transmute them to Divine Love and

Light and restore me to my highest vibration. Fill all voids in my energy field with Divine Love and Light."

If you know from whom you received the unwanted energy and the nature of the energy—such as fear, anger, or sadness—then you can add the person's name and energy to the prayer. It could go like this: "Divine Beloved, please clear from me this (feeling or sensation) that I received from (name). Transmute it to Divine Love and Light and restore me to my highest vibration. Fill all voids in my energy field with Divine Love and Light."

You can disconnect yourself from discordant energy or another person by imagining you are unplugging a cord from them and saying, "Divine Beloved, please disconnect me from (name or energy) and reconnect me into my higher self." Imagine you are plugging this cord into the chakra above your head. Now imagine you are unplugging cords from your body and say, "Disconnect everyone and (energy) that are connected into me and reconnect them into their respective Higher Selves." Imagine the cords disconnecting from you and going back to their source.

13: Sensing the Anima-Spirit

Let's use your empathic and intuitive talents to deepen your awareness and connect to the life around you. The more self-aware you become, the deeper you connect and can engage with the world and its living beings in an impactful way.

Imagine yourself in the Heartland Forest. The Heartland is full of life: the pool before which we sit, the ground we rest upon, the fire that warms us, the animals, the birds, and the trees.

As mentioned previously, in the Calming the Mind breathing practice, take some deep, cleansing breaths. Inhale to the count of four heartbeats. Exhale to the count of six heartbeats. Do this several times, calming the mind and body. Calming the mind allows you to sense subtle forces and receive messages.

Keep breathing and notice how your breath affects your body. Feel the effect on your body and how the ground supports you as you inhale. Feel the effect on your body and how the ground supports you as you exhale.

Allow your awareness to expand so that when you exhale, you settle more deeply into the earth. Imagine a strong cord running from the base of your spine, deep into the earth, tethering you to a golden ring deep in the core.

Allow your awareness to expand, touching everything around you, bit by bit. What do you notice?

Do you sense life around you?

Do you sense a presence, a spirit around the trees, the animals, the fire, the pool, and the birds?

Do you perceive how they all fit together in perfect harmony and Divine Order? That each has a place and a purpose, and each is a necessary piece of the great puzzle?

When you feel the connectedness of all that is around you, come back to the present moment.

What insights and inspirations did you receive?

Did you get a sense that each plant, animal, and element has a spirit and is a piece of the Goddess?

Try talking to the plants and animals as if they could hear and understand you. They do. See what happens.

Allow the Goddess to speak to you. Awaken to your special talents. Strengthen your understanding that you are a physical expression of the Divine and her blessed child.

 ## 14: "Feel It"

Let's try an experiment called "Feel It." It will help deepen your understanding of other life forms.

Find a place to sit, preferably outside in nature. After calming your mind with the breathing practice, take a minute or two to notice the surrounding life. It might be a crow or robin looking for food, a squirrel running along a branch, or your pet. Choose one to be the focus of this exercise.

Take more slow, deep breaths, inhaling to the count of four heartbeats and exhaling to the count of six heartbeats. As you exhale, imagine your feet rooted into the ground. When your mind feels calm, imagine you are the life form you chose.

What do you notice? Avoid judging what you feel. Allow yourself to become the life form's body. Let your mind become their mind.

What do you feel?

What message does it have for you? Their message may be a new awareness of yourself and your world.

What else do you notice?

Come back to your body and take a few cleansing breaths.

Repeat the process with a tree of your choosing. What does it feel like to be a tree?

Do your roots go deep into the ground, anchoring firmly into the earth and grounding you? Let your awareness travel up the tree like life-giving sap, reaching for the heavens.

What do you notice?

Do you feel the ancient wisdom of the tree, sense its experiences over the decades and centuries it has lived?

If the tree could talk, what message would it have for you?

Come back to your body and take a few cleansing breaths. Repeat this practice as often as you want with rocks, plants, animals, the earth, people, and objects. It doesn't matter if it is animate, like an animal, or inanimate, like a rock or soil. Everything has a spirit. Allow yourself to become it by shifting your awareness. Ask your subject if it has a message for you.

Review what you noticed. How hard was it to allow yourself to dissolve into another presence?

What was it like to become something or someone else?

Did you notice everything is alive?

Could you feel its spirit?

Could you sense its purpose? Perhaps with the tree, you felt like a bridge to the heavens, strong and firmly anchored in the earth. The message could be: "Stand tall and strong."

What wisdom from this experience can you apply to your current life?

 ## 15: Consciously Receiving From Another Lifeform

When you are ready to experiment, find a willing friend, pet, or plant. Be sure to get permission from your friend.

Before you start, notice how you are feeling.

Are you anxious?

Are you worried you won't be able to do it or do it right?

Are you scared to reveal what you might notice?

And, heaven forbid, what if you are wrong and make a fool of yourself?

Rest assured. It's okay. The first time you start something, it's bound to be awkward and haphazard. If you are worried, practice with your pet, a tree, or a plant. They won't judge you.

Practice: Sensing a Plant or Pet

Allow your mind to relax and your body to be supported by the ground.

Breathe into your heart by placing your attention on the heart area. Allow your heart to expand by feeling grateful or appreciative of something. When you feel your heart swell and have a sense of peacefulness, shift your attention to the plant or pet. Automatically, you touch the other's energy field.

Allow yourself to notice visual or other sensory cues, such as the smell, color, and stature of a plant, body language, or facial expressions of your pet. These are all useful tools that work with your unique way of receiving information.

Ask simple questions:

Are you thirsty?

Are you hungry?

Do you need more light?

Do you need to go outside?

And any other questions you might think of that require a simple yes or no response.

Notice how you get your answers.

Do you simply know?

Do you feel them in your body, such as feeling thirsty or having a gut response of yes or no?

Do you hear your plant or pet speak?

Or get an image?

This is your primary way to receive. It is your gift.

Practice: Sensing A Friend

Get permission from your friend before you attempt to read them.

As described previously in the breathing practice, inhale and exhale slowly and deeply, allowing your mind to calm and your body to be supported by the earth. Breathe into your heart by placing your attention on the heart area. Allow your heart to expand by feeling grateful and appreciative of something. When you feel your heart expand and have a sense of peacefulness, shift your attention to your companion. Automatically, you touch the other person's energy field. At first, it may be easier to do this practice with your eyes closed.

Listen with your senses for a few minutes. What do you notice?

Ask your friend to tell you something that she has experienced. As you listen, don't let your mind stray to what you will say or how to solve her situation. You are listening with all your senses, and your mind is not engaged except to observe.

Notice the tone, cadence, speed of narration, and word choice. Listen deeper. What is not being said?

What do you sense about your friend? Is she happy, sad, angry, or excited?

How do you receive this information?

Do you feel her emotions? See images, hear or smell something, or just know?

Tell your friend what you sense. Invite her to share her experience.

Often your friend will validate what you picked up. But sometimes, she will not want to reveal and acknowledge what you sensed, or she may be oblivious to what you perceived. Don't let that undermine your confidence. Take a break and do it again or with another person. Soon, you will tune in consciously to the emotions and physical signs of another.

As you refine this skill, you will sense your friends without them saying a word. You will learn to read his or her energy field by sensing it with your increasing intuitive talent.

As you practice receiving, you will learn to separate your own feelings from the emotions or sensations of another. One of the easiest to identify is anger, which often masks fear. But first, you must discern where and how you feel anger in your body.

Do you get a knot in your belly or a surge of heat that puffs you up?

Or do you get impatient with your animal friends?

When you feel physical sensations without cause, it may be another person's energy. Alternatively, another person's energy can activate an unresolved trauma that causes you to become angry, sad, or fearful.

A word to the wise: It is spiritually unethical to invade a person's psychic space and probe into their energy field without their consent. Under normal circumstances, it is best to ask before you read another's aura. That being said, you will pick up energy from people. Just notice and don't judge. Don't share unless invited or unless the situation is life-threatening. When you do share, be compassionate and respectful. Preface your information with a phrase like, "Do you have any questions for me?" or "May I share something I'm sensing?" When someone invites you, your words will have a greater impact.

SELF-REFLECTION PROMPTS

How has your empathic nature been a gift and tool?

Do you find yourself more receptive to visual or auditory input?

Or does touch communicate more deeply to you?

Is your body highly responsive to physical sensations?

Do you simply know things?

Can you intuitively smell a rat and know when someone is trying to deceive you?

Have you noticed times when you were excited to do something, but when you had time to think about it, you wish you hadn't agreed?

Do you feel other people's pain in your body?

Do you feel other people's emotions?

Do you sense your spirit?

Do you feel connected to your spirit?

How would your life be different if you knew everything had a spirit and a purpose?

How would you approach life? Would you feel you were never alone?

How do you nurture yourself and practice self-care? Do you spend time alone, and enjoy restful quiet? Do you receive massages and take baths? Do you engage in uplifting activities and with positive people?

What can you do to shift your perspective and see your empathic gift as your best friend?

What thoughts and beliefs must you let go of to fully embrace your empathic nature?

If your empathic gifts were in service to you, what would your life look like?

How would you use your empathic gifts?

Sometimes we can become weighed down by the "stuff" we collect, like the Dawbird in the next story.

LETTING GO TO BECOME MORE

The Dawbird and the Crow

A flash on the forest floor attracted Dawbird's attention. She swooped closer, circled, then landed a few feet away. Cocking her head to one side, she strutted around the shiny object several times, peering at it with one eye, then the other. Loud caws alerted her of Crow, who had followed her.

"He always wants what I find," she grumbled. She snatched the silver pin and winged it away before Crow could see what she had found.

Returning to her nest, she carefully placed the pin among the other treasures she had accumulated. She fed her babies. Before she left to search for more food, she covered them with leaves to hide them and the bits of metal, glass, copper, silver, and gold coins, nuts, and flowers that filled her nest.

Every day she went off to forage for food and treasures. She brought them home and added them to her nest, which had become so heavy that the branch it rested on drooped ominously.

Crow watched Dawbird. He envied her collection of incredible finds. Even though they were not edible, he coveted the metals when they glistened in the sun.

Dawbird watched over her nest and chased off any thieves that dared to come near. As time passed, the limb sagged so that if she added any more items, the nest would crash to the ground, and she would lose everything.

One day, Crow came to Dawbird and said, "Let me help you with your nest. It will fall, and your babies will not have a place to grow. You have so many things in it. Let us build a bigger and stronger nest."

"You just want to get your beak on my treasures," she said, ruffling her feathers. "I know your kind. You are unscrupulous thieves." Even as she protested, her nest shifted on the limb.

"Let me help you, Madam Dawbird. You don't want years of collecting to be lost in the forest duff."

"Go away, Crow. My nest will stay just where I put it."

Crow consulted with his cronies. "We could just let the nest fall," they suggested. "Then we can salvage all she has gathered and take it for ourselves."

"I have a better idea," said Crow. "We must make her think we are not interested in her nest."

The next day, Dawbird woke to a ruckus of repeated *caw caws* retreating into the distance.

"I wonder what happened?" Dawbird said. She listened and watched. "With Crow gone, I can enjoy my time hunting for treasures today." She covered her little ones and flew off in search of food and whatever else she could find.

Crow watched from high in a tree. One crow followed Dawbird, flying from treetop to treetop while the rest converged upon her nest. They collected everything they could carry. Soon, Dawbird's nest was empty except for her hatchlings, which the crows had covered with leaves.

A short while later, Dawbird returned, carrying a shiny white pebble with red streaks within its translucent core. As she dropped her prize into the nest, she gaped in alarm. "I've been robbed!" she cried and wept.

The next day, she spied Crow. She fluffed her feathers and flew circles around him.

"You stole my treasures. I spent years gathering those bits. You have no right to take what is not yours."

Crow shook his head. "See, your nest is safe again, high above the ground. We did you a service. What if your nest had fallen in the middle of a storm? You would have lost everything, including your chicks."

Dawbird screeched at Crow. "You have ruined my life, taken everything that I valued. Each item in my nest held a memory."

"Look at it this way. All those things you had collected were weighing you and your nest down. Now you can fill your nest with new things that match what is important to you now and don't hold you in the past."

Dawbird stared at Crow. "You don't understand. Those treasures define me. They were as much a part of me as my feathers." She turned her back on Crow. "Go away, Crow. I never want to see you again."

Dawbird settled into her nest to grieve her loss, ignoring her chicks. Her gaze settled on the new treasure she had found today.

"I will gather more treasures. Different treasures. I will make my nest more magnificent than before."

THE HEALER'S PATH: ELLARA'S WISDOM

Letting Go to Become More

How many times have we clung to old treasures, belief systems, or possessions, even though we know underneath, they overfill and threaten to topple our life? Like the Dawbird, we get furious when someone comes along and forcibly takes what we have been hoarding, even if it is best for us in the long term.

Old habits run deep and often are invisible to us. To truly change, we must let go of some things that have been near and dear to us. This could be food, a companion, sex, euphoric herbs, or any number of things that we use to make ourselves feel good. When we overly rely upon these things to the point of distracting ourselves from our true calling, they become a detriment to our personal evolution.

We have patterns of behavior that we hide, such as getting angry, becoming afraid, or telling ourselves we are not good enough or deserving of something. We may leave a relationship to avoid the pain of betrayal and abandonment or drive ourselves to make a comfortable nest that we think is safe and secure. It's easy to become complacent, settle into an unsatisfactory status quo, and avoid the change that is needed.

These coping patterns often start as ways to reconcile inconsistencies in childhood. Investigating the roots of these behaviors is often fruitful.

Sam was my comfort during my childhood, and it was easy to depend on him. His visits were the pinnacle of my life. After we hand-fasted, we made a safe nest, something that I had longed for during my childhood. He protected me. We enjoyed an intimate connection even after the children were born.

Change comes unbidden. The signs of a wasting illness were there for several years, but I pushed them aside, hoping Sam's health and the shadow disturbing the hearts of Albans would miraculously resolve. I didn't want to change. But Alba changed. Clerics aggressively hunted and killed Healers, putting me in danger. I wanted to do something, but I was afraid. Sam became my excuse. I rationalized I needed to protect him because it helped me to feel safe and avoid what I most feared: being alone in an unsafe world.

But the Goddess had another plan for us. She gently—or not so gently—prods people to fulfill their destiny, as she did me. Sam died protecting me from capture in the skirmish with the Natuan soldiers at the Sheldon docks. My comfortable, safe life shattered, and the battle was thrust upon me. I would not have chosen to become more than I was. After all, I am a proficient Healer. Why did I need to become more? However, my destiny is bigger than being a local Healer, and circumstances prodded me forward. (Author's note: You can read more about Ellara and Sam in *The Rebel Healers*.)

Before stepping into your Goddess-given role, you must release certain things from your life. Some things you are happy to let go of, such as a trying childhood, work that doesn't set your heart on fire, and people who make you feel small and inconsequential. Letting go of others who are close to your heart is more painful.

As heart-wrenching as it was, there was a purpose and blessing in Sam's sacrifice. He taught me what I needed to know in order to move onto the next level of my destiny. It is unfortunate that he could not continue the journey with me. However, I feel his presence assisting me from the other world. The rebellion in Sheldon and the deaths of Sam and my friends galvanized me to act. They forced me to step more completely into who I am and discover that I am more than I once thought myself to be.

Sometimes, we need something powerful to break us free from our comfortable life to become who we are meant to be.

Circumstances, such as an unplanned career change, caring for a partner or parent, or an accident or illness, can cause us to grow and make changes. Sometimes we choose to change, which is the less painful and preferred method. But unplanned and unwanted events push us to evolve faster, force us to tap into our courage, and hone our talents to discover that we are greater than we currently perceive ourselves to be.

It is all too easy to grow complacent in a relationship that feels predictable and safe. Or a profession that puts food on the table but doesn't fill the belly of your heart with joy.

Becoming more means facing your fears—the need for safety, letting go of broken trust, fear of success or failure, fear of rejection, and fear of being unlovable.

We are all Goddess-born, yet something inhibits us from becoming visible and powerful.

You are much more than you think you are.

Letting go of something that has served you for a long time is hard and takes a patient, gentle hand. Releasing what no longer supports you sounds onerous but is an important part of any transformation. The old and outdated must go so there will be room for the new. It is a requirement if you want to fully embrace your highest potential.

I invite you to spend time with this concept and look at your daily life. What kind of self-talk is shaping your behaviors and your body? What is the energy of the people that surround you?

Applying Ellara's Wisdom

Releasing the Past Daily Practices

16: What's Working and Not Working List

List what is not working in your life. These could be times when you feel obligated, where you are afraid to say no or yes, situations that make you fearful, tense, or that sap your energy, and so forth.

Next, write down what you enjoy doing.

Determine how much time you spend doing each item on your list.

What do you notice?

17: Fire Ritual

From your list in the previous exercise, write something you want to release on a piece of paper. On a separate piece of paper, write what you would like to replace this with. For example, you might want to release the need for overly serving someone or of holding back your feelings of anger and resentment toward someone. You would write this on one piece of paper.

Since releasing creates a hole in your energy field, you will need to fill it with a positive attribute so that the old belief or behavior cannot easily return. Take a few minutes and imagine what you would like instead. Be sure to word it in the present moment and in a positive format. For our example above, on the second piece of paper, you could write, "I empower (person's name) to take care of themselves." "I am in touch with my feelings and freely express them." "I forgive (person angry at), and I am at peace with (person angry at.)" Or "From the depths of my heart, I love and accept (self or another person)."

Light a candle or build a small fire. It can be more effective to do this outside during a full moon.

Take some deep breaths to calm your mind and spirit. When you feel ready, call forth the spirits of the four directions.

"Thank you, Spirits of the South, and Grandmother Serpent, for helping me shed the old so that I may be healed and rebirth a new way of being.

"Thank you, Spirits of the West, and Grandmother Jaguar, for helping me explore the deeper meaning of (whatever it is you are releasing) and find the hidden treasures there.

"Thank you, Spirits of the North, and Grandmother Hummingbird, for bringing stillness so that I might discern the wisdom from (whatever you are releasing) and wait for the right timing to do the impossible.

"Thank you, Spirits of the East, and Grandmother Eagle, for showing me, with great clarity, my path forward and the best way to express myself.

"Thank you, Spirit of Mother Earth, for giving me form that I might serve.

"Thank you, Spirit of Father Heaven, for giving me life, that I might fulfill my destiny and bring glory to the Divine."

Ignite the paper with what you want to release, saying, "I release (whatever you are releasing) to the Spirit of Fire. Let Fire transmute (whatever you are releasing) to Divine Love and Light."

Next, refill the vacant place you have created in your energy field. Read your positive statement, then also burn it, saying, "Let the Spirit of Fire warm my heart with (whatever you said) and fill me with Divine Love and Light."

18: Letting Go Journey

Calm your mind with your breathing.

Step into your heart awareness by breathing into your heart and feeling it expand.

Keep breathing as you imagine yourself walking into an ancient temple. Make your way to a large chamber where there is a broad stone altar.

As you approach the altar, you notice items on the stone. A guardian spirit stands to one side. She points to the altar. "These are new opportunities for you. What do you choose?"

Allow your intuition to guide you to something that resonates with you. It could be a color, a fragrance, a sound, an item, or a being. You know this is for you.

The guardian notices what you are drawn to. She says, "To take something new, you must give up something that no longer serves you. What are you willing to let go of?"

Listen for a response from your body or an inner knowing.

Decide if you are ready to give this up. If you are not ready to let this go, it's okay. You can come back when it is the right time. If you are ready, then imagine placing what you surrender onto the altar. It could be a belief, a responsibility, a person, or a behavior. Imagine what that item would look like. As you place the item on the altar, thank whatever you have been carrying and are now releasing.

Collect the energy that is offered to you.

When you are ready, thank the guardian spirit of the temple and return to the present moment. Take time to integrate the new energy into your body and life.

Self-Reflection Prompts

If you could do anything, be anyone, live anywhere, and have all the resources you needed, what would your life look like?

Where would you live?

What would you do?

Who would you do it with?

Now ask yourself, what is holding you back?

Is it fear of not having enough money?

Or safety?

Or fear of what your partner or others would think of you?

Are you willing to stand up for what is important for your well-being, even if you go against the status quo?

Do you fear rejection, abandonment, ridicule, or being called lazy and irresponsible?

What change can you make in your life that will take you closer to your dream, your ideal life that fulfills your heart's desire?

Can you delegate a task you don't like?

Can you communicate your needs more openly? Perhaps you have the courage to be vulnerable with your partner and share your deepest desires. Maybe it is taking time for yourself to do things that fill you with life force and joy.

What have you given up to fit in or appease others?

How has that worked?

Are you healthy but constantly tired? That is often a sign that something is out of integrity with your heart. It could be a person, an energy, a belief about yourself or your life. It is an invitation to let go.

What are one or two small behaviors you can change today so you can shift to doing more of what you love?

You are priceless, precious. What you do and who you are in this life reflect the tapestry that is you. Each person has his or her own tapestry, complete with rich colors and scenes depicting her specialties.

THE TAPESTRY OF DESTINY

The Crow and Grandmother Spider

Crow cocked his head and peered at the sparkles between the trees. "This is unusual," he cawed to his friend.

"We've never been to this part of the forest," his companion replied. "Let's take a closer look."

The birds flew from tree to tree, cautiously approaching what looked to be a giant spider's web. Sunlight filtering through the treetops made the dewdrops dance on the fragile strands.

Crow landed near an elderly spider who formed a network of webs with her front and back feet. Crow watched her with one beady eye, then the other. Finally, he addressed her. "Grandmother Spider, why are you not spinning your web in the customary way? And why is it so expansive?" He extended a wing, indicating the tree some distance away where the other side of her web connected.

The old spider didn't stop weaving and moved along her web as if she had not heard him.

Crow hopped along the ground below the web, which stretched from the forest duff halfway up the trunk of a tall tree. He noticed flies trapped in the sticky silk, along with seeds, bits of leaf, animal hairs, earthy threads, and dandelion puffs.

"Grandmother Spider, your web has flaws. It has trapped all manner of items. Why do you allow that?"

Grandmother Spider paused and studied the crow. "You are young. You think in absolutes. It is good. It is bad. It is black. It is white. You have an idea of how a web should look because most of the webs you have encountered are made a certain way." She returned to her weaving. "When you get older, you will see that life is not about trapping bugs to eat. You see the beauty in what you have created."

"But with all those seeds and leaf bits stuck on your web, it doesn't look beautiful."

"Son, it is the random seeds, the unplanned debris that the soft winds blow into the web, that turn the ordinary into the extraordinary. Into a magnificent tapestry." She grasped more gossamer threads from old webs and shaped them with her feet.

Crow shook his head. "It looks like a mess to me. You are wasting your time and effort."

"Without the random bits of debris that land on my web, there can be no tapestry. With them, it becomes a web of destiny. The things that stick to it make it interesting. Fly to yonder tree and tell me what you see."

Crow and his buddy flew to a distant tree. As dappled sunlight touched Grandmother Spider's web, it shimmered like translucent silk. The bits of foreign materials appeared to be placed perfectly to form patterns and images. Crow watched for a long time, mesmerized by the shifting motif as the light breeze and sunlight touched it.

He returned to the spider. "You are right, Grandmother Spider. What seems like blemishes close-up become beautiful patterns from a distance." He glanced at his crow friend. "Aren't you afraid someone will destroy this work of art? What if we accidentally flew through your tapestry?"

"I would be sad to see such a masterpiece destroyed. But other tapestries will survive." With a leg, Grandmother Spider pointed to other spiders who created their own masterful webs of destiny.

THE HEALER'S PATH: ELLARA'S WISDOM

The Tapestry of Destiny

We each have a role to play in our world and a specific purpose, a specific destiny. As we understand our true nature, we understand the threads of our destiny. Our true nature is our destiny.

Those steeped in the wisdom of the stars say that the time and the place of your birth show the path of your destiny. The planetary influences at the moment of your birth represent the themes of your personality and your personality type. You might be an impatient, fiery person, or you might be a sensitive, emotional person. You might be a keen thinker with a quick, nimble mind or you might be a workhorse, rock solid with feet firmly planted on the ground. But there is more to you than what is contained in the energies of the stars under which you were born.

The essence of the Goddess, otherwise known as a soul or our spirit, animates our bodies. Our soul has desires. It wants to explore and have experiences. Often, the soul plans events so that it can gain lessons and wisdom.

Some souls are part of an interdimensional team of spirit warriors, wisdom keepers, and light-bringers, much like the Leonini Guardians and the Gra'Bandia Healers.

The soul's agenda often includes opportunities for personal growth and participation in grander opportunities to evolve humankind, the planet, and all life forms. Even the chaos in our world today is an invitation to evolve our consciousness.

Unlike our ego, the soul accepts what we experience and in whatever form that takes. But our ego likes to have things unfold in a certain way. Planetary influences define egoic tendencies at the time of our birth, as well as from the energetic imprints and beliefs we develop in our childhood.

This planet offers its citizens free will and the ability to choose. The question is, what are we going to choose? Or do we choose to believe we are fated on a particular path?

Let me speak for a moment about fate and destiny.

Fate is what happens when we live our lives believing that we don't have the freedom to make choices and that things, events, situations, and people "happen" *to* us. It's a way of avoiding responsibility for your life. Often, it is much easier to let someone else decide something for you. Then you have someone to blame, like Rokan, who blames Garrick and the old Grand Master for a choice forced upon him. But Margot points out that he could have made a different choice, and if he had, his life would look very different. Not making a choice is also a choice.

Often those things that "happen" are perceived as something negative, something undesirable, something that's fixed with no other options available. Rokan doesn't think there is a way out. He thinks this will be his existence, his fate, until the day he dies. He doesn't acknowledge the options he has and rejects any new ones for fear of the consequences.

Do you see how easy it is to get caught in the trap of thinking you don't have a choice? You unconsciously abdicate your ability to choose because you don't think you have a say, so you live life by default.

That is fate running your life. Fate is not having a choice. Fate is not claiming sovereignty over what happens. It is believing you are dealt only one hand of cards and have only one roll of the dice, and that's just the way it is.

Destiny has a different energy.

Destiny comes from believing you have options and from consciously deciding. These choices may or may not work out as expected, and that is alright. When you understand you chose a particular path and take time to evaluate the results, you are in a powerful position to course correct. You make a different choice that might result in a different outcome.

Destiny is about making choices that lead you on your personal heroine's journey by using the wisdom you've gained, along with your gifts, abilities, and talents. This journey is an invitation to learn, grow, and expand upon what you are capable of and apply your wisdom to a cause that is usually bigger than yourself.

Fate has few options, which often leads to living your life in narrow ruts. Destiny expands your awareness beyond the confines of those ruts and brings about personal growth. It serves the greater good of the community and the world in a significant way.

Destiny is about choosing to share your special gifts and talents unique to you, with society, with your neighbors, and with your family.

This sounds simple. But before you can fully understand your destiny, you have to understand yourself. Your destiny includes the conscious expression of your natural, soul self.

I never thought about fate or destiny until it was thrust on me after Sam died, and I was alone and hunted. Sam and Nana Magog hinted, but I ignored them.

Nana came to me where I grieved Sam in the glen. "Get up, Child," she said as she poked me with her cane. "It's time for you to know the Goddess's plan."

I protested, but Nana ignored me.

She said, "You can't deny your life's mission. Your destiny will find you no matter how fast or far you run from it."

I scowled but settle onto the log. I take a deep breath. "Alright, Nana. What do *you* think is my future?"

"Listen carefully, Child. You were born when the Goddess required Her Healers to restore the balance in our world." She shifted on the piece of wood. "The Dark Lords of the Tiarna Drocha feed upon our world's fears and misery. Their agents, the Droc'ri sorcerers, do their best to create chaos, disrupting countries and people's lives to satisfy their shadowy masters. You already know the Grand Master means to destroy the Goddess, Her servants, and every Goddess-born they can find. He thinks he will then have unlimited power with no one to stop him. In his ignorance, he thinks he will rule the world. In reality, Gea will become another domain of darkness upon which the Dark Lords feed. The Grand Master believes Alba is Her last stronghold. He has already started undermining the Goddess's protection, and Alba is crumbling."

"How can we stop it?"

Nana continued as if I had not spoken. "The taint of the Tiarna Drocha has invaded Alba, destroying the harmony that has existed in our society for centuries. The source of it must be rooted out and touched by the Light of the Goddess."

I leaned back, shaking my head. "This taint is like a shadow without form or location. How can one fight a shadow? Especially one from another realm that is very unlike our world? Wouldn't it be better to tackle something with substance, like the Natuan invasion or the king?"

"That's why it's time for you to receive the Gra'Bandia Council's blessing and step into your legacy."

"I just want to eradicate the Natuan mercenaries and their influence. How will the Council's blessing make things different? I already channel the Goddess for healing."

Nana snorted. "That's child's play. You have the talent and ability to become a human host to the Goddess. The Voice of the Goddess. You can become part of a Triune like your mother, and I were. You *must* have the Council's blessing to do that."

Reluctant as I was, at least she gave me some direction and a starting point. Destiny is a very personal path.

Destiny's Path

As children, we see people and admire them. We might try to be like them, but often, that falls flat. There are certain aspects you might emulate, and that may awaken some of your own personal gifts and talents. But the problem is, another person is not you.

I didn't know this until I was much older. As a young person, I wanted to be like Nana Magog because she seemed to be powerful and she was free to go places and had magic. I couldn't do the things she did.

Interestingly, some people challenge you, and you will resist them. Like Nana Magog. It frustrated me how she wouldn't respond to my questions. I was determined to find answers, and her uncooperative behavior made me hunt for them. Even after I learned to restore others to health, it frustrated me that I couldn't do magic. What I didn't understand was that I did have magic. It just didn't look the same as Nana's or the other Healers at Cuilithe.

When we compare ourselves to other people, we go astray. If we think we need to be like someone else, we create a limitation on ourselves and it becomes harder to recognize what is special about ourselves.

You are like a tapestry of a beautiful scene. You may have to observe the entire picture from a distance as Crow did. Like the debris on Grandmother Spider's web, our experiences make us and our life journey unique. Interactions with people help you see sections of your tapestry. By paying attention to the qualities you like and dislike in the people around you, you can get to know more about your personal tapestry.

Understanding what you don't want is also a way of revealing your unique thread. It helps you know what's not yours.

Self-discovery will allow you to take back your power to choose. When you know what nurtures and supports your well-being, feel your connection with the Goddess, and have access to your ability to hear the whispers of your soul, you become a force to be reckoned with and a threat to the dark forces. Inner certainty transmits a high-frequency vibration into the world that brings positive change.

The only person responsible for your life is you. If you let other people guide your life, you abdicate your Goddess-given power to choose. You quietly slip from treading the path of your destiny to being trapped by fate.

APPLYING ELLARA'S WISDOM

Weaving Your Destiny Daily Practices

19: Understanding the Bigger Picture

Calm your mind with the breathing practice outlined in prior chapters.

Imagine yourself standing before a huge loom with a vast line of threads. With each pass of the shuttle, an image emerges. You notice the strands and the patterns are in different colors and shapes, and from your vantage point, you witness a bigger scene take form.

Imagine you are one thread in the loom. Pick one and follow its course. Notice how it weaves between other threads, forming new patterns, and shifting the colors in a section. Don't analyze it. Just notice how, as the weaver reveals the tapestry and as you follow your thread, you move in and out of scenes, patterns, and colors. Like a thread in a tapestry, you weave in and out of people's lives, situations, and relationships.

Can you see how your thread becomes a necessary part of the tapestry?

What would the tapestry look like if your thread was not there?

Take a moment and honor your role in the bigger picture. Without you, the tapestry would not be complete.

 ## 20: Who You Wanted To Be As A Child

As children, we still remember our soul's mission. As we get older and we are told to stop being silly, we bury these soul desires.

Calm your mind and ground your energies with the breathing practice.

Think back to your young days. What did you want to be when you grew up? It could be to care for animals, heal people, be a warrior, or do other endeavors.

What does your soul want you to do?

What does that look like?

Where would you do that?

Contemplate your answers. It may take a few tries to really connect with your soul's desire, and that's okay. Your soul and your spirit team of helpers give you what you are ready to hear at that moment. When you are ready for more, they reveal a little more of the tapestry.

21: Refining Who You Are

Find a quiet place where you can connect with your inner self. Calm and ground yourself with the breathing practice.

Make a list of the things that you're naturally drawn to. For example:

Do you like to study?

Do you like to analyze economics?

Are you curious about science?

Are you drawn to animals?

Do you like to work with your hands and build things?

Do you like to go deep into existential philosophies?

Do you like to work with other people?

Heal them, teach them, lead them, guide them?

Are you a storyteller?

What do you do regularly?

Look back over your life and see what patterns emerge.

Scan your list. What are common themes? What talents have you developed?

22: Anchoring Who You Are

Make a list of things you like to do that you enjoy and are fun.

Is there any overlap between this list and the one from the previous exercise?

Now, take this list, and as you read through it, notice your body's responses. Ask yourself:

Is this something I like to do?

Or is it because I think I'm supposed to do it?

Is this something I like to do because it pleases another person?

Are you doing this to make money?

Is this something I like to do because it feeds my soul?

Let's take this one step further. Beside each item listed, jot down why you like doing it.

What part of you does it fulfill?

What talent are you using?

If something you think you like is coming from your head, notice how your body feels. Does a part of your body become tense, or tighten up, or do you get a knot in your stomach or throat? Or other signs?

Notice how your body comes alive and your heart opens and expands when doing what you love aligns with your soul's nature. If you feel full of life, that is a way to tell if this is part of your true nature.

Since our minds can easily override our heart's wisdom, let's approach this from another angle.

Have a friend read these questions and your answers to you. Notice how your body responds.

Or better yet, have your friend or a family member or your boss say, "I want you to do (whatever it is you wrote on the list)," and see how that feels. We trick ourselves all the time with our minds. The real test is if someone asks you to do something on your favorites list. For example:

"Will you draw this picture for me?"

"Will you write this story for me?"

"Will you teach this?"

"Will you heal me?"

"Will you give me a massage?"

"Will you do this onerous task?"

"Will you do..."

Notice how your body feels. Are there conditions, such as does it depend on the person and the situation?

If there is any doubt, if there is any uncertainty, if your heart says maybe, consider scratching those things off your list and out of your life.

On the other hand, if you feel alive, invigorated, and your heart expands, that can be a sign you are on the right track.

A word to the wise. Sometimes something that is actually part of your soul's desire won't resonate with you. There can be several reasons for this. One is that it is not the right timing. Another is that fear blocks it. This could be fear from other lifetimes where you had a traumatic experience, such as being tortured and killed for this gift. Another reason can come from beliefs engendered in childhood. If you encounter this phenomenon, it's all right. The seed has been planted, and as you grow and evolve, you will welcome it.

Self-Reflection Prompts

To what degree are you living your life with an attitude that your fate is fixed and you have no control over your life?

Do you believe that you have a choice in what happens in your life?

How does it feel to deny your soul's desire and serve others out of obligation?

Does it feel like someone stole your power?

How much of your childhood dream are you living?

What have you learned about your true nature and destiny through the exercises?

To what degree do you understand you are a divine soul being and that by choosing to express your true nature (your soul being-ness), you are living your purpose and destiny?

Do you know the role you play in restoring harmony in our world?

Are you living your destiny?

I want to impress upon you that you are special, that you are unique and important. You don't have to live up to other people's expectations. As you work through this book, you will gain insights into yourself and see this truth for yourself.

Feel free to repeat these exercises a few days, weeks, or months later. Notice if there is a change.

Embracing Your Innate Power

The group before me is quiet. During the days we have been working together, we have increased in numbers, and now there are campsites dotted all over the glen. It reminds me of Cuilithe, only smaller. And no hawk-faced Doyen Camila.

"Connecting to your heart's wisdom is critical to the journey upon which we embark and the challenges which we face. Current circumstances invite us to see through the illusions around us, drop the facades we have used to navigate our world and remember and reclaim what we have put aside.

"Leaders operating from their shadow sides have perpetrated their wasteful, greedy, and manipulative practices on our world for long enough. It's time to think for ourselves, see through their illusions, and make innovative choices. Whether we accept it or not, we must undertake this heroine's journey. It is up to us to play our part in global rebalancing and restoration.

"Now that you have experienced more of yourself and the invisible—yet very alive—part of your existence, you can take this new wisdom with you into your daily life and into your outer world experience. Developing an intimate understanding of yourself and of your inner life lays the foundation for navigating the outer world.

"Like navigating the treacherous currents of the outer island archipelago of Alba, it is easy to get swept away by what's going on in the world and in your life. Before you let your emotions make your decisions, stop, take a few deep breaths, and ground yourself. If it is not a life-or-death situation, take time to ask yourself what's really going on. Step back so you can see the bigger picture. Then, you can decide what is the best choice and not decide based on default behavior or flawed information. Make choices that not only support yourself but benefit others as well. Have the courage to set boundaries with the certainty that you are respected.

"This is often easier said than done. Distractions abound: delays brought about by unusual weather patterns, disagreeable people, failing economies, or deliberate deceptions by others. No matter whether you live in bustling cities, a small town on the seacoast, or on a farm, start noticing the world around you and make small, sustainable choices that support you and our world. Pay attention to the results of your choices.

"Seek the truth in every situation. Ask questions and use your intuition to see through illusions and the plots to destroy our freedom and autonomy. Use your discernment to make supportive choices.

"Let Divine inspiration guide you into more sustainable decisions that respect all life forms and the planet we call home. You will know whether they are the best choices by how you feel and the results you witness. If you feel enlivened, your heart expands, and your body relaxes, then you are on track. When your body tenses, your heart constricts, energy trickles, and you feel tired, the situation is not healthy and supportive. It is an invitation to step back to gain a different perspective and make a different choice."

I stop before the central fire and look up. The first rays of dawn dim the pinpoints of light in the indigo sky and caress the treetops. Songbirds sing salutations to the new day.

"Remember your native abilities and talents.

"Live close to nature.

"Create and live with true equality in your relationships.

"Be free to follow your heart in occupations that fill you with vitality.

"It is time for us to step into our innate power and sovereignty—to bring the changes needed.

"Thank you for your willingness to explore yourself and your relationship with life. I hope you have received insights and are inspired to reclaim that part of you that was set aside or hidden.

"We are the rebel healers and way-showers, the ones who see through the smoky illusions of the dark forces, who think for themselves, and who make choices that take the best of the past and create a sustainable, peaceful future. A win-win for all.

"It is our state of mind, our level of consciousness, and our reflection of the Divine that will allow us to prevail and not be overthrown by the machinations of the agents of the dark forces. Remember, you are Goddess-born and here for a mission.

I wish you an inspired journey.

Ellara, Rebel Healer

ABOUT THE AUTHOR

Elaine is a seed planter, a light-bringer, and a member of a group of light beings whose mission is to transform the way people see themselves, humanity, and their role in our world. Connected to other realms, she encourages one to connect to their Divine Self and live out their soul's mission.

As an activator, she uses her channeled stories and other channeled creations to help one remember what has been forgotten. She works with a group of multi-dimensional, high-vibrational light beings whom she calls Alena-Sophia.

From childhood, Elaine's dream was to heal people with a thought. But she didn't know how, nor was there anyone to show her. Given psoriasis at a very young age, she started on a lifelong journey of exploration and remembering. In search of a cure, she progressed from conventional Western medical treatments to traditional Chinese medicine.

Realizing the source of her malady was beyond the physical, she branched into ancient sciences and spiritual teachings, shamanic practices, indigenous healing, and energy techniques, as well as Astro-Numerology, Human Design, Soul Realignment, and much more. She realized that her Soul Self was using the stubborn skin condition as a catalyst to urge her to step into her destiny.

Liberating herself from social expectations, she surrendered the life of business and finance to focus on becoming the healer she writes about in her stories.

You're invited to experience some of the creative downloads that come from Alena-Sophia. Start with *The Rebel Healers* and this companion guidebook. If you would like a personalized session with Elaine, you can go to www.elainec.com.

Acknowledgments

The essential oil practices are Elaine's adaptation of the teachings by Tiffany Carole.

The Fire releasing ritual is an adaptation of Dr. Alberto Villado's teachings.

For more information on empaths, go to www.hsperson.com for research by Dr. Elaine Aron.

Other Books by Elaine

THE REBEL HEALERS Series

The Rebel Healers (Book 1)

The Kurat Curses (Book 2)

Brush with Death (Short Story)

Flight to Alba (Short Story)

Tales of the Leonini (Inspirational Fables)

Lessons for the Goddess Born (Companion Guidebook)

DECODING THE SOUL Series

Numerology, Your Monthly Oracle

The Tao of Yahtzee

If you enjoyed these stories, please tell your friends. Leave a review and help others discover the book.　　www.elainec.com

Illuminating Inner Wisdom

Printed in Poland
by Amazon Fulfillment
Poland Sp. z o.o., Wrocław

30301280R00107